Me and My Shadow

with love

Derek

Extract from 'Phenomenal Woman' from AND I STILL RISE
by Maya Angelou is reprinted by kind permission
of the publishers, Virago Press

'Warning' by Jenny Joseph from SELECTED POEMS,
Bloodaxe Books Ltd., Newcastle-upon-Tyne.
Copyright © Jenny Joseph 1992

HarperCollins*Publishers*
77–85 Fulham Palace Road,
Hammersmith, London W6 8JB

A Paperback Original 1995
1 3 5 7 9 8 6 4 2

A catalogue record for this book is available
from the British Library

ISBN 0 00 638438 2

Set in Galliard by Rowland Phototypesetting Limited
Bury St Edmunds, Suffolk

Printed in Great Britain by
HarperCollinsManufacturing Glasgow

This book is dedicated with love and gratitude to Staff-Nurse Trubshaw and the magnificent team at the Royal Marsden Hospital. Also to the memory of my beloved brother, Robert Lloyd Hamilton-Hill.

O Rose, thou art sick!
The invisible worm,
That flies in the night,
In the howling storm,

Has found out thy bed
Of crimson joy;
And his dark secret love
Does thy life destroy.

    — William Blake

Acknowledgements

Firstly, I would like to thank Colin and Anna Haycraft without whose encouragement and enthusiasm I might never have started this book.

I would also like to thank all those who helped me through my illness and supported me while writing this book: Annabelle Geddes, Stephen Pickles, Jeremy Brett, Jennie Barke, Patrick, Andrea, Shirley and Cynthia Hamilton-Hill, Sandy Fawkes, Mark Colivet, Jemma and Tim Owen, Luke Redgrave, Corin and Kika Redgrave, Rachel Kempson, Crofton Cooper, Louise FitzGerald Burden, Peter Scaramanga, Bridget Armstrong, Trisha Edwardes, Sue Locke, Geoffrey Aquilina Ross, Jeffrey Bernard, Dr Barrington Cooper, Dr Eleanor Shaw, Diana Hanbury, Angus and Joyce James, Richard Crabtree, Christopher Roberts, Ros Watkins, Penny Gordon, Polly Smith, Ruby Landry, Pippa Whittington, Dawn Booth-Clibborn, Jonathan Benson, Barbara Rennie, Cecilia Moynahan, Eva Hardy, Pia White, Mark Herne, Guy Blackburn Hamilton, Clive Graham, Johnny Summers, Kate Eldridge, Simon Rothman, Michael Rothwell, Liam Kelly, Sophie Nelson, Charles Johnson, Danae Brook, BJ and Bernadette Lingham, Joan Hughes Bonk.

Thanks also to Robin Saikia who metaphorically held my hand from word one to the final full stop.

Thanks to my agent Caroline Dawnay, and my editor Val Hudson for their invaluable advice and friendship.

A very special thank you to Sam and Jim Kher, the proprietors of my local corner shop, The Hollywood Deli. They kept me supplied with food and drink, and allowed me to run up bills that would have embarrassed Wall Street, always trusting that one day, my dire financial situation would improve.

Finally a special thank you to Doreen Tagoe who patiently transferred my badly typed manuscript on to her word processor, saying how much she enjoyed it, thereby lifting my sometimes flagging spirits.

Contents

1
Shock

God grant me serenity to accept the things I
cannot change, courage to change the things I
can, and wisdom to know the difference.
– *Reinhold Niebuhr*

The consultant entered my cubicle. He had the lined, friendly
face of an old and trusted country doctor. I had no fear; I was
quite confident that I was not ill. He smiled compassionately
as he said, 'I am so sorry, my dear, your biopsy has proved
positive. You have a malignancy in your left breast.'

I just stared at him. I wondered how many times before he
had delivered a potential death sentence, and whether he ever
got used to it. I felt rather sorry for him. The shock was too
great for me to start to think about myself and my feelings.
All I knew at this moment was that my life would be changed
for ever.

A nurse came into the cubicle. 'Time for your blood tests,
dear,' she said. I could hardly understand what on earth she
was saying. She repeated the words.

I looked at the consultant and dumbly shook my head. 'I'm
sorry,' I said, 'but I need to be alone right now. Would it be
possible for me to come back tomorrow and see to all that?'

'Of course,' he replied gently. 'Of course you need a little
time to take all this in.' I was free to leave, to come to terms
with one of women's worst nightmares.

*   *   *

I had gone to see my GP some weeks before with a lump the size of an egg in my left breast. I had been lazy about the well-publicized self-examination technique, and this was the result. I knew it was extremely important to have it looked at immediately. I am normally a ditherer – even an ostrich; after all, who needs bad news? But this time I moved quickly.

'A nodule,' my GP had said and I was only too happy to believe him. But I looked up 'nodule' in the dictionary: 'a small knot, lump or node', it said, and I realized that in no way was my lump small. So I asked him to arrange an appointment at the Royal Marsden Hospital, my local, just to make sure. I wasn't worried. There was no history of cancer in my family, and many friends had found lumps all over the place which had proved to be benign.

So it was with great confidence that I set off for the Royal Marsden Breast Clinic one beautiful spring morning in 1991. I was accompanied by a close friend, actress Gabriella Licudi, with whom I was working on a book. Our synopsis had been accepted by Sidgwick and Jackson, and we had received a nice advance that was keeping the wolf from the door. The book was entitled *How to Survive After Thirty-Five*, something we had both become experts at: we had lived through a whole spectrum of situations and been rich, successful, stony broke, on the dole, divorced, single parents, and yet we had survived to tell the tale. Looking back, I realize that we talked about everything *except* my appointment. How great the weather was . . . the latest book we were reading, last night's TV – anything that took our thoughts away from the impending examination. The only way we could tackle the subject was by deciding to take notes on this new experience by way of research for our book. We had been through many of the negative aspects that come with growing older, but cancer was a blank slate.

The clinic was a bright, friendly place. There were booklets scattered around explaining that in most cases lumps in the breast were indeed nodules, so, armed with this information, I signed in and went out into the yard for a smoke with Gabriella. I noticed that the yard was littered with cigarette butts and wondered how many fearful women had paced up and down puffing away to relieve the tension. Not me, though: I wasn't afraid. Gabriella and I decided that once I was through we would go out for lunch, give up work for the day, and start again the following morning.

My name was called, and I went to have a mammogram. This is a technique used in the early detection of cancer: the breast is examined using X-rays. I was taken to the X-ray department, having exchanged my clothes for a surgical robe. The technician was extremely friendly and allayed any fears I might have had. I had already had a mammogram the previous year which had proved clear, and I was convinced that I would still be OK.

I sat waiting for the result, chatting about this and that with the other women in the queue. I became rather irritated because although I had got there first, I was the very last to be called into the surgery. Did I smell a rat? No, I did not. How stupid can you be? How *dumb*? It simply did not occur to me that I had been kept until last because there was something seriously wrong.

Well, now I knew: I was suffering from cancer. *Cancer!* I dragged my clothes on, and went out into the yard, where Gabriella was waiting for me.

She took one look at my face and tears started rolling down her cheeks. We stood there hugging each other, not knowing what on earth to say. I mean, what *do* you say? My first thought was that I needed a drink – a big one – so with that in mind, I steered us towards Finch's, our Fulham local. But how could I face people? How could I face people when I was in shock . . . when I felt that my life was about to fall to pieces? I could hardly join in the genial chit-chat of my friends there – I was in no fit state. So we stopped at the local off-licence instead and went back to my flat.

We drank a bit and tried to talk to each other, but we were both uncomfortable. I was now in the land of the halt and the lame, and Gabriella in the land of the healthy. The slightly forced smalltalk in which we had previously taken refuge to avoid 'facing the issue' was impossible to sustain now. The cat was well and truly out of the bag, and there was no way back. I entertained the idea of drowning my sorrows, but realized that it would take a crate to calm me down.

Gabriella understood my need for solitude and left. I was very grateful.

I paced up and down the drawing room, smoking like a chimney, not knowing quite what to do or what to think. What *should* one think? There were no signposts in this new country – no comfortable clichés to clutch at. Everything seemed unreal. The day had dawned like any other but now my safe world was upside down. Everything had changed. 'I am suffering from cancer,' I told myself over and over again. 'I am very seriously ill.' It made no sense. There was no pain, no visible sign of anything wrong, yet there was a dark malignancy inside me, gnawing away at my life. I went to the bathroom and looked in the mirror, almost hoping to see some tangible sign of the illness. Pace, pace, pace, pace, my brain in total panic.

In the grocer's shop over the road, where I went to buy more cigarettes, I looked about me in a paranoid way, wondering if other people could tell. 'Lepers used to wear bells round their necks,' I thought. 'Perhaps I should.' I started laughing to myself, remembering that the last time I had worn a bell round my neck was during the summer of love in the sixties. I felt guilty laughing. This was no laughing matter; it was deadly serious, and I felt I was being irreverent and flippant in the face of this terrifying reality.

4

A friend came up to me in the street. 'Deirdre,' she said, 'there is something I have been dying to talk to you about.' *Dying* – the word leapt out of the sentence at me like a smack in the face. How could anyone use that word in so trivial a context? I soon learned that even the most innocuous conversation now had its trip-wire – it was a minefield to be negotiated. There was so much that I had to learn to find my way through this new world.

By the time I got home I was shaking and crying. I couldn't stop. It was as if a bomb had exploded in my brain. The last time I had been near a hospital was to have my children. But how different things had been then – inside me a blossoming of life, a wonderful miracle; now I was carrying an evil, destructive thing which would be my loathsome companion wherever I went. The awful reality was beginning to sink in, and fear was taking over. I was trembling so much I could hardly light a cigarette or pour myself a comforting drink. I was going to pieces. I sat for a long while, head in hands, sobbing away, while I frantically racked my brain for what to do next.

I knew that if I telephoned close friends or family for comfort in this state I would panic them. I needed a professional counsellor, someone accustomed to the initial shock of people who have just been told they have cancer. I calmed down enough to look through the phone book for cancer help-lines, and found CancerLink, an organization set up as a counselling service for cancer victims and their families.

When I got through I was crying so much I could hardly speak, but a calm, relaxed voice soothed me and I managed to explain my plight. Her tranquillity in the face of my hysteria was a great relief. This was exactly what I needed – someone who was not fazed by the word 'cancer'. My helper explained to me that she once had felt just like I did. It was wonderful not to feel so acutely alone any more. Serious illness does make one feel cut off. This is why support groups are so important – you realize that you have fellow sufferers and that you are all in it together.

'You must think in a positive way,' the voice continued. 'It will help your recovery to be calm. Be resolved not to let any negativity into your life.'

Recovery! *Recovery?* I had not even thought about that. I had assumed that mine had been a death sentence. *Recovery!* What a wonderful word it was. It made me cry more, but with relief. At last I had a signpost in my world of chaos. Hazy it was, intangible, but it glowed gently in the distance.

When I finally put the phone down, my thinking had been transformed. People did survive this dreaded thing. I realized that I would have to undergo chemotherapy, a possible mastectomy, perhaps radiotherapy – all sounding so scary – but if they led to *recovery*, so what? I didn't dwell on the thought of losing a breast: just then it was a case of 'my kingdom for a horse'. That was something I would deal with if and when necessary.

We all find the very word 'cancer' (astrological sign apart) quite terrifying, but I think that I was especially ill equipped to deal with it. The word was avoided at home when I was a child. I would ask my mother what was wrong with a friend of hers, and she would roll her Irish eyes upwards and say that he or she had got 'the unmentionable'. The *unmentionable*? What could she mean? I was about eight when she first used the expression to me and had just finished reading a book about the bubonic plague, so I naturally assumed, with absolute horror, that carts would soon be coming round in the depths of night and we would hear, 'Bring out your dead! There's plenty of room on the cart. Bring out your dead!'

Years later, when I lived in Chelsea, we would sometimes drive past the Royal Marsden Hospital. My mother would look at it, giggling nervously, and say, 'I always have the feeling that a great hand will come out of one of the windows and pluck me in.' We would drive on, guiltily savouring the knowledge that there were poor people in there with *cancer*, but we were 'All Right, Jack'.

Well, I certainly wasn't 'All Right, Jack' any more. The great hand had got me. It was with Mum's denial in mind that I decided to be honest with people and tell them the truth – that I had cancer. This would help to demystify the word and divest it of its awesome power – for my own benefit as much as for that of others. I know that some people prefer to keep it a secret and let only their immediate family know the truth, but I think it is better to talk about these things and dispel the conspiracy of silence.

Do you remember those old films where the family and doctor gathered outside the patient's door, discussing whether or not they should tell him the truth? Well, this luxury of choice had not been mine. On the contrary, *whack!* straight between the eyes, and once the shock had subsided I was grateful for it.

I rang family and a few close friends, and told them my news. Now that I was coming to terms with the idea, their reaction came as a surprise. Two burst into tears. Flowers, cards and plants began to arrive at my flat. I was just beginning to experience the great network of love and support that would sustain me. My friend Louise was marvellously helpful. She had suffered from different illnesses all her life and had faced them bravely. She knew about being ill – about the isolation it brings – and put me in touch with friends who had been through the same ordeal. It was so reassuring to hear their laughter and encouragement and to think that my life might one day be normal again like theirs.

My ex-husband Corin Redgrave was a great source of strength. Initially I was very nervous about telling our children. How do you tell your offspring something so ghastly? Corin reassured me, and I knew they had him to lean on. Our daughter Jemma was twenty-five, already a highly acclaimed actress. She was rehearsing Thornton Wilder's *Our Town* with Alan Alda. Our son Luke was twenty-three and, having trained as an assistant cameraman, he was about to depart on a back-packing journey around the world. They were, of course, terribly upset, but so full of love and optimism that they lifted my spirits. I would fight this thing, if only for them. It was a help that they both had such exciting projects to occupy them, and their youthful confidence in my strength to overcome this dreaded illness reassured me.

I returned, as instructed, to have blood tests. How strange it felt. The day before it had never dawned on me that I was to be a patient. Now I felt I was separated by a lifetime from my previous carefree attitude – 'To hell and back', as Audie Murphy once wrote. But the kind and caring manner of the nurse assigned to guide me through the afternoon's ritual helped me to leave behind the trembling little mouse and to be strong and dignified.

Thus far I had done what had to be done. I had had the blood tests, told family and friends, and to a certain extent stopped panicking. Now it was time for me to find my courage and take a long hard look at who I was and what I had become. My life had been so full of activity that I had neglected that quiet part of myself that needed to blossom in solitude and meditation. I needed time to think.

For the next few days I experienced an adrenaline rush – rather as if I had taken an illegal substance, or been hit by the restless energy that comes with falling in love. I paced and paced. I awoke early, full of trepidation, unable to sleep.

So it was that I took myself every day to our local park, Brompton Cemetery, to walk off the angst. This might sound morbid, what with the intimations of mortality and all, but it is a beautiful, peaceful place, full of great trees, flowers and wildlife – the nearest thing to nature in my neck of the Chelsea woods. I took nuts for the squirrels, who were quite tame and would come right up to me, and bread for the birds.

It was indeed a beautiful spring: bluebells and other wild flowers grew in profusion, and the old grey gravestones were covered in mosses and ivy, reminding me of that passage in *Wuthering Heights*: 'I lingered around them, under that benign sky; watching the moths fluttering among the heath and hare-bells, listened to the soft wind breathing through the grass, and wondered how anyone could ever imagine unquiet slumbers for the sleepers in that quiet earth.'

How soothing it was, how healing. How it focused the mind far away from the ever-present worry of self. The silence, apart from birdsong and rustling grasses, comforted me, and the earth smelt sweet.

One morning I found myself sitting opposite a gravestone with the inscription:

> So young without care or thought
> She did far more for others than she ought,
> She stayed her post, the fire to beat
> Till God called her to one deep sleep.

It was the epitaph of a Margaret Bryant, who had died at the age of fifteen. How brave she had been, how selfless. The words inspired me: if she had been capable of bravery and selflessness aged fifteen, then so, aged fifty-two, was I.

There was one epitaph that always amused me – that of one Thomas Cole (1800–1867), late of Kensington:

> Spectators all as you pass by
> As you are now so once was I,
> As I am now, so you must be
> Prepare for death and follow me.

What an old sod he must have been, wanting to spoil everybody's day.

Anyway, the question I had to answer remained: Was I afraid of dying? *Yes!* Some years ago I came across an interesting statement by Beryl Bainbridge in the *Sunday Correspondent* magazine. Asked how she would like to die, she replied, 'Wearing clean underwear.'

This made me think. As a good convent girl, I had always been taught that to be hit by a ten-ton truck and mangled to death was as nothing compared to the horror of being hit by a ten-ton truck and mangled to death if not wearing scrupulously clean underwear. The logic of this escaped me since I assumed that what with being mangled and all, no one would be able to tell the difference. Then I wondered how I would answer the question put to Beryl, and decided my answer would be: 'When I have come to terms with it.' Which made me realize that I had not yet managed to do this.

It had been a long time since I had really thought about all this. My life was so active, so full of incident, that contemplating death was simply not on my list of priorities. At convent school you never thought about anything else, but you did so with a happy pragmatism. It was no big deal. All would be well for you as long as you didn't lie, cheat at exams, swear at the nuns, throw the disgusting convent food round the room (something that happened quite often), steal, kill or, worst of all, become an adulteress. Sex, at that age, was simply not a force to be reckoned with, so I did my best not to cheat at exams, only swore under my breath, and felt smugly that on the 'life after death' front I was doing quite well, thank you.

This self-satisfied attitude changed somewhat while I was at my convent in Rome. We were studying Dante's *Inferno* in Italian and, with my new-found interest in boys, it scared the pants off me. One Sunday afternoon I was allowed to take myself off to the cinema because I told them I was going to see *The Song of Bernadette*. Total lie. My girlfriends had talked about the wonders of Marlon Brando in *The Wild One*, which was banned in England. It was the first biker film. Well, that was it: I sat through it three times running and knew that Dante's *Inferno* had been invented for the likes of me. How could you concentrate on essays when all you wanted in life was to be on the back of Marlon's bike? *Any* biker's bike! The wild side of life beckoned, and how was I, aged sixteen, equipped to reject it?

I was not sixteen any more, and my biker dreams were long gone. I was fifty-two, I faced a life-threatening illness, and I was frightened of dying. It was time to tackle all this, and I set about trying to rekindle the embers of my religious faith. I had a great well of spiritual knowledge to draw on, having been educated at the Roman Catholic Convent of the Sacred Heart – first in Malta, where I grew up, then in France, and finally at the beautiful Mother House, La Trinità dei Monti, at the top of the Spanish Steps in Rome.

After the war, my father (a virtual stranger to me at that time) left the Royal Navy and took a job as director of Rediffusion on the island of Malta. When I first arrived it seemed very strange to me. I was used to green fields and leaden skies in England; here I was confronted by a riot of colour, honey-hued sandstone houses, bright blue skies and an emerald sea. What a wondrous and healthy place to grow up. I learned to swim, play tennis, water-ski, scuba dive, and ride; I even attempted polo until one day I swung my stick too high and nearly knocked myself out with it!

It was a childhood spent roaming around barefoot in the sunshine, and on hot summer nights I would sleep on a lilo on my balcony and gaze sleepily at the canopy of iridescent stars, dreaming whatever it is that little girls dream of. We lived in a beautiful villa overlooking the sea with a large garden full of honeysuckle and bougainvillaea. A child's paradise.

During the war I had been a lonely only child. One of my most terrifying memories of the war was something that took place when I was three. My mother had left me in the charge of her cleaner as she set off on her bicycle to order an Anderson Shelter: bombing raids were getting ever closer to the cottage in Hampshire where we lived. (My father was away in the Navy.) While she was gone, the air-raid siren shrilled out, and the cleaner panicked. She started screaming, then flung me into the cupboard under the stairs, followed by her young son, then herself. She closed the cupboard door, and I lay in the pitch black for two hours while she alternately screamed and vomited all over me.

My mother was aghast when she returned to find the three of us, crammed in the cupboard in a state of shock. She told me later that for ages I would not let her out of my sight because I had been so traumatized. Eventually however, at the age of four, I was packed off to a boarding school in the country to get away from the bombing. Jane Eyre at Lowood.

Many years later when, suffering from claustrophobia, I was seeing a shrink, I recounted this story, experiencing once again the terror I had felt. I started shaking, sweating and crying, for the first time letting the fear sweep over me because I felt in safe hands. It was an immense relief, but I can't help wondering how many similar experiences one has blocked out – experiences that only return in nightmares, as they did for Hamlet: 'Oh God! I could be bounded in a nutshell, and count myself a king of infinite space, were it not that I have bad dreams.'

Another war incident gives an insight into my mother's character; she and I were in the wine cellar of a stately home, which served as the household's shelter, as the sirens roared around. My mother saw the old matriarch of the family trying to push her way out. Alarmed, Mum tried to stop her, asking why she needed to get back to the house.

'Because I've left my false teeth on my dressing table,' replied the old lady.

'Well, you won't be needing them now,' said Mum. 'They're dropping bombs, you know, not sandwiches!'

No matter how dire the situation, my mother never lost her Irish sense of humour.

Now, in Malta, I was no longer lonely. I made lots of friends and, for the first time in my young life, I possessed what I had read about in books: two parents – a mum and a dad. How fine that was! And to add to my happiness I soon had two brothers. Now we really were a family.

The Maltese people are open hearted, warm and welcoming like the Irish, so we settled there happily. It was in Malta that I first came across racism. One day I was on a bus returning home for lunch from the beach. The bus was full of Maltese people apart from two English women sitting in front of me. In voices like foghorns they were saying how stupid the Maltese were – their servants in particular. I went bright red with embarrassment and nervously looked round, but the other passengers just sat there with dignity, pretending they had not heard the insults. I loved the Maltese and identified strongly with them. I crept off that bus, ashamed to be English. My parents were conservatives and expected me to share their views, but, looking back, it was incidents like that bus journey that precipitated my gradual trek towards the Left.

Malta was a marvellous place to grow up: endless parties, nightclubs where you danced under the stars, evenings spent on beaches around a fire, with people playing the guitar. One of our favourite sing-along songs was 'Just Walking in the Rain' (a hit for Johnny Ray), a bit of an anachronism given the sweltering heat. Romance was ever in the air accompanied by a lot of fifties-style heavy petting. It was easy to fall in love at least once a week. Then the Suez crisis blew up, and regiment after regiment, ship after ship steamed into Valletta, ready to go on to Suez if necessary. My friends and I were swept off our feet: we felt like Deanna Durbin in *One Thousand*

Men and a Girl. It was a magical time for all of us there, but not perhaps the best preparation for dealing with the harsh realities of life.

The first time I went to school in Rome my mother made a mistake and sent me to a different order, St Joseph's. She also dispatched me there two weeks before term started. I was furious, thinking of all the good times I could still be having in Malta. To others, my mother's vagueness was all part of her Irish charm, but being forced to lose two weeks' holiday did not endear her to me. Moreover, I discovered that having spent years as a Sacred Heart girl, coming into another order was like arriving on the moon.

Anyway, I turned up at this run-down establishment, speaking little Italian, enraged at my plight, to find that the only girls there were orphans who lived with the nuns full time, and who had, to put it mildly, a weird sense of humour. That first evening they explained to me in pidgin French that I should follow them as they had a surprise for me. How nice, thought I. Oh yeah! They led me, blindfolded, down endless corridors. I realized at last by the echo on the tiled floor that we must have entered a large room. The girls knelt me down and ran off giggling, saying that I must remove my blindfold when they gave the signal. I did as they said and found that I was kneeling in front of the chapel's altar: to my horror I saw that my nose was two inches from a pane of glass which separated me from a neon-lit dead nun. I thought I was going to have a heart attack! I closed my eyes and prayed with all my might. The nun's flesh was dark brown, which contrasted startlingly with her starched white wimple. Oh, God, where had Mother sent me? My terror occasioned great hilarity among the orphans, who came and patted me on the back, saying what a good sport I was. They little knew what murderous plans I was hatching for them!

I prevailed on my mother to remove me from this hellhole as soon as possible, and departed for the Trinità dei Monti, feeling safe once more in my familiar order.

Unlike many of my friends, I thoroughly enjoyed life in the convents: I was good at languages and learnt fast. At La Trinità dei Monti our special treat was to have tennis coaching by the Italian ladies number three. I was good at tennis, and although I never managed to take a set off her, it was often a close-run thing. I enjoyed the theatre and mystery of the Latin Mass, and like many young convent girls I decided that not only did I wish to become a Catholic, but also a nun.

Writing this, I can imagine a tidal wave of derisive laughter from my friends and acquaintances. But at that time in my life, it was true. We were taught that there were only two options in life for us: to have a family, or to take Holy Orders. I had two younger brothers, and had observed at close quarters what a lot of trouble they were; how much more alluring were the quiet, secret mysteries of the cloister.

There were one or two contradictions, though, in the lives of the nuns. For example, I always found it curious that when a nun died, the other nuns got in a frightful state about it. Why should this be, when according to their belief she had gone to embrace her Bridegroom? Wickedly I imagined to myself that they were jealous because she had got to Him first. And since all the nuns died of old age, they were clearly wanting in the attraction stakes. I wondered if perhaps, on the other side, they would appear to Him as young girls. Surely He wouldn't want a clutch of old nuns hanging around, especially when some of them were cruel and horrible. I resolved to die young and be His most pale and beautiful bride of all. Numero Uno. It was all a great mystery!

'Seek and ye shall find,' it says in the Bible, so I sought and sought. I started by going to my local Catholic church, lighting candles and praying as hard as I could. I felt a complete fool because I was so totally unfamiliar with the ritual. Boredom set in, and I found it hard to concentrate. I remembered that in my convent days prayer had been a delight to me, and I determined to resurrect my spiritual self: it must, I felt, be lurking about somewhere in my unconscious.

A dear friend and very devout Catholic, Anna Haycraft (the writer Alice Thomas Ellis), once explained to me that whatever doubts one might have, however impossible faith might seem in our increasingly violent world, the most important thing was to keep on praying, no matter what. I looked up the word prayer in the dictionary, and in the long explanation I came across: 'prayer is our solution to human problems'. That seemed perfect. I prayed for courage – not for my life, that seemed selfish, but for the courage to handle whatever lay ahead. I had now accepted my cancer. I was not fatalistic; it was simply that I had come to terms with the fact that I had it. 'Acceptance' is a key word in these matters. Once you have accepted something unpleasant, however difficult it might seem at first, it frees you to deal with it. No more wringing of hands; no more attempts at denial – you just face the problem head on and fight it. I found that by adopting this attitude the road ahead looked less daunting.

Helen Keller, who became deaf and blind at only nineteen months, wrote: 'I have never believed that my limitations were in any sense punishments or accidents. If I had held such a view, I could never have exerted the strength to overcome them.'

Now that I had acceptance and prayer on my side, the next step was positive thinking. This started off in a curious way: the odd snatch of a song would come to mind, for example Monty Python's 'Always Look on the Bright Side of Life', or 'Pack Up Your Troubles'. Then I recalled that I had bought 'I Will Survive' by Gloria Gaynor when going through a disastrous relationship, and had played it over and over again to regain a crumb of self-esteem. As Noël Coward once said, 'Strange how potent cheap music can be.'

I sang those songs to myself while stomping around Brompton Cemetery. Then I got it! It was so easy, really. If singing 'Always Look on the Bright Side of Life' could help, then think of all the books, films, poetry, music and religious works I had at my disposal! Nothing negative, mind you.

Years ago I went to see a film called *Cries and Whispers* by Ingmar Bergman. It was deeply depressing (when isn't he?) because it was centred around a young woman dying of cancer. There is one horrific scene when, after she has died (or so I hoped) of the dreaded illness, she suddenly sits up (despite being dead), tears falling from under her closed eyelids, her disembodied voice describing the awful process of dying. I nearly jumped out of my skin. After all the suffering she and the audience had endured, surely she would be only too pleased to be dead. But Bergman was never one to let you off lightly. Oh no! He'd already done me over in *The Seventh Seal*. It was ages before I could relax happily in woodland without imagining Death stalking through the trees. So Bergman was definitely off my list – him and Samuel Beckett.

I also recalled a televised Oxford Union debate on the existence of God. John Mortimer, maintaining that God didn't exist, won the debate. It was in my wavery religious days, so I kept hoping he would lose, rather as he had lost in court when Corin and I had paid him to defend a black friend of ours, accused of sedition. But no chance. The result had upset me and I realized now that, being so impressionable, I must only take on board ideas that suited my philosophy.

My list of things *not* to do grew longer: not to read anything by Sylvia Plath (I recalled saving a neighbour's life: she had just finished *The Bell Jar* and was halfway out of her window!);

not to listen to anything by the gloomy Leonard Cohen (who would want to anyway?); not to read Revelations in the Bible (you're scared enough already). It was, I suppose, a form of self hypnosis, but I didn't care. Out of the window went debate, doubt, conflict of beliefs, and it worked!

My religious scepticism was partly a typical convent girl's rebellion against her years of indoctrination, and partly a change brought about by the strong influence of my atheist husband Corin. I admired his intellect so much. He had been educated at Westminster, and had gained a double first in English at Cambridge, so what he said went! All my education had made me fit for was to say 'Hail Mary's' in English, French, Italian and Latin, play good tennis, and do fine embroideries. I did not understand then that spirituality has nothing to do with acquired knowledge or that being an intellectual can be more of a hindrance than a help.

Although Corin had agreed to get married in a church he teased me mercilessly when I headed for the Brompton Oratory on a Sunday. Slowly but surely he undermined my strong faith, and it left me feeling like a small boat which has slipped its moorings and is being tossed about on a threatening sea. I know he did not want to upset me, merely to broaden my horizons, but I wasn't ready for it. Discussions on religion were part and parcel of our early married years, and eventually I learnt to hold my own.

In the sixties Corin and I went to see a film called *Ma nuit chez Maude*. It was one of those typically French films *très philosophes*, centred around a debate between two friends, one a Catholic, the other an atheist, on the validity of their different ways of seeing the world. After much tribulation and agonizing the atheist concluded that it was, on balance, better to have a faith because if you died and the whole thing wasn't true, you would never know. Living with faith is comforting;

living without it makes the whole exercise somewhat pointless. I was much heartened by *Ma nuit chez Maude*.

But how could I have gone and married an atheist? At my convent in France the nuns would get us to pray for a dreadful Englishman who lived on the French Riviera, writing blasphemy. This was W. Somerset Maugham. In their eyes he was on a par with Judas Iscariot, and we girls would get hold of his books and read them with delicious terror lest his ideas contaminate us.

Years later, I occasionally had lunch with another famous atheist, Francis Bacon. He would always turn the conversation to the question of faith and, once I had overcome my shyness of the great man, I was very surprised by his interest in what I had to say. It wasn't that he wanted to change his views in any way: he had no fear of death, and he could certainly have found a savant to guide him if he so chose. It was more that he was mildly entertained to find that there were still people with my views around, especially in Soho!

It was about two weeks after I had learned about my cancer that Jemma brought me a book called *Love, Medicine and Miracles* by an American cancer surgeon called Dr Bernie Siegel. It introduced me to the practice of visualization – an absolute *must* for anyone with cancer. What happens is that you make a mental picture of your cancer in any form you like (I used the image of a horrible dark purple jellyfish), and then imagine it being blasted away. I was feeling too sensitive to want to kill anything, even my cancer, so I visualized the jellyfish being transformed into a shining white light which gradually evaporated.

Every spare minute of the day was spent perfecting this technique – standing at bus stops, doing the washing up, before drifting off to sleep. Time spent on the most trivial of tasks was no longer wasted as I was able to use it in a positive way. This helped me to feel that I had a degree of control over my destiny and over my unquiet mind. It gave me something to hang on to. In my moments of panic – now, thankfully, much less frequent – I used the exercise as a soothing mantra.

Having gone through shock, and reached some kind of acceptance of my illness, it was now time to face a new trial: chemotherapy.

2
Coping with Chemotherapy

Slowly the poison the whole blood fills.
– *William Empson*

Three weeks after my diagnosis I went to the Marsden to start a course of chemotherapy which they said would last six months. For all my meditations in Brompton Cemetery, my attempts at visualization and singing 'Always Look on the Bright Side of Life', when the day dawned my stomach was churning with fear. I had seen the newspapers – the photographs of bald celebrities, the horrific accounts of the sickness, and knew I was in for a rough passage.

I had been told about people who simply put their foot down and refuse it under any circumstances – in fact I had read in a survey that eighty per cent of doctors and nurses would not entertain the idea. However, I did not have the courage to go against the specialist's advice: I knew that I was being treated at the finest cancer hospital and under the best supervision. I was fighting for my life here, and what they said went. After all, who was I to gainsay them?

My daughter Jemma came to collect me, and took me out for lunch in the garden of an Italian restaurant. The day was sunny and the breeze cool, and we laughed and talked about anything but my appointment. Jemma regaled me with

21

anecdotes about her rehearsals with Alan Alda who was helping her a lot with her role. She was very enthusiastic about the play and working with him. She had already had marvellous notices for her performances in Strindberg's *Easter* and Arthur Miller's adaptation of Ibsen's *Enemy of the People*. She had played leads on TV and in films, but classical theatre was her passion.

There was a tension in both of us, and I gulped down the chablis like there was no tomorrow. This lunching out was to become a ritual, and I had always felt rather guilty about it until just recently when I read an article in the *Sunday Telegraph* by George Pitcher about his wife's chemotherapy. He wrote: 'I have vivid memories of that period. I remember how we would get howlingly drunk in an Italian restaurant across the road [from the Marsden] before each increasingly harsh chemotherapy (drinking wasn't going to make her any more violently sick).' At least I was not the only one who partook of Dutch courage.

Once I had gone through the obligatory blood tests, Jemma and I sat holding hands in the queue waiting for chemo-therapy. As I looked around, my worst fears were confirmed. At least half the patients had lost their hair. Some women were wearing obvious wigs, or had wrapped scarves around their heads. The young men looked OK – as if they had adopted the style as part of their youth culture – but the young girls, so vulnerable about their appearance, looked very sad. At my age, how dare I worry about hair loss?

Chemotherapy is treatment with cytotoxic (which literally means 'cell-poisoning') drugs. There are thirty cytotoxic drugs, which destroy cancer cells by interfering with their ability to grow and divide. Chemotherapy, unlike radiotherapy, is a whole body treatment: the cytotoxic drugs circulate in the bloodstream and can destroy cancer cells in different parts of the body. The most common method of administration is an injection into a vein using a syringe or a drip. They may also be given as tablets or capsules.

Eventually it was my turn, and Jemma and I went into the chemotherapy unit. The male nurse was kind and courteous. 'I am now going to inject the drug into your hand,' he said. 'The first thing that you will experience is a tingling in your bottom.' He then produced a syringe full of dark blue liquid. It was huge! It looked as if it could stun a herd of bison.

I proffered my hand and looked away. It didn't really hurt and I was surprised when he said, 'That's all for now, Deirdre. See you in three weeks.' The fact that he called me by my first name was reassuring in this alien land. So with my tingling bottom, and the pills from the pharmacy to help combat the sickness, I went home.

I waited and waited to feel something unusual, my senses on red alert for any changes. They came soon enough. I started vomiting daily, and felt sick all the time, much as I had when I was pregnant. My taste buds changed: I could not tolerate the idea of spicy or garlicky foods; everything I ate had to be bland and boring. Alcohol, in my case wine, became undrinkable, but a clever friend who had been through chemo told me that if you wanted a drink, vodka was the one to go for. He was right! Another side effect was constant tiredness, and an inexplicable feeling that I was living on a different planet to everyone else.

The time had come for my son, Luke, to depart on his backpacking adventure round the world. I had strongly mixed feelings about this. Of course, I had all the worries that mothers have when their child departs to God knows where: Will he be safe? Will he get some awful disease? Will his plane crash? He was travelling with a very solid and nice young man which reassured me a little. I was excited for him but I was going to miss him – and would I be here when he got back?

Before he left, he taped himself reading meditations and visualizations from Dr Bernie Siegel's *Love, Medicine and Miracles*, backed with whale songs. He also gave me his Walkman to play it on. It was a great comfort to me to listen to his dear voice as I imagined him having the adventure of his life in strange and wondrous parts of the world. Friends whose offspring had gone back-packing said that the best advice they had was to take loads of condoms and not to carry dope across a frontier! So with that excellent counsel ringing in his ears, Luke left. Jemma and I saw him off at Heathrow, and as I hugged him goodbye I felt an overwhelming rush of emotion. I hadn't wanted to cry but I couldn't help it. How handsome he looked! How I would remember that moment over the months to come.

I worried about Luke's travels, but he was very streetwise, partly from having misspent an unfortunate two years at Holland Park Comprehensive.

He had arrived home from school one afternoon to find me playing the record of Pink Floyd's 'We don't need no education, dark sarcasm in the classroom', and was so furious that he broke it, saying he needed an education and wasn't getting one. I had liked the teachers and the ethics of the school, which had a very good record for art and music, two of the subjects that Luke excelled in, but he suffered from the lack of individual attention. On top of this, it came to my attention that some parents were going to the school to buy drugs from the pupils. I decided it was time for a change.

I found a charming minor public school in the Cotswolds, all I could afford, and Luke thrived there. Indeed, he gained as many 'O' levels as Jemma, who studied at Godolphin and Latymer, a very academic girls' school. Corin disapproved strongly of the public school system, but let me have my way on this.

Luke was a dreamy child who lived much of the time in his

imagination. I had bought a set of luminous stars which shone when the light went out and stuck them on his ceiling, and he loved to lie on his bed – looking up at his 'sky at night' and listening to music. While he liked his door shut when he went to bed, Jemma liked hers open in order to be in touch with what was going on. They were completely different.

Jemma and I were very close. She had always been so wise. When she was little and I shouted at her she would say, 'Mum, don't shout at me. When I am naughty I need you to hug me.' That made sense. I remembered one occasion when Corin and I had just bought a carpet for our drawing room, and were expecting friends for dinner. The room looked perfect, quite elegant, and flowers and candles added to the atmosphere. Then Jemma, aged six, knocked over a glass of red wine on to the brand-new carpet. I started shouting at her for being clumsy: 'Go and fetch a cloth to clear up this mess!' I yelled. Well, she just stood there looking at me eyeball to eyeball, one hand on her hip; with the other, she picked up the bottle and, never taking her eyes from mine, poured the rest of the contents on to the floor.

I stood there, completely stunned. How could she have the effrontery to do such a thing? I was totally nonplussed. Then I understood what to do. I picked her up and hugged her, telling her that I loved her so much. I understood that she was telling me she had not meant to spill the wine; in the great scheme of things, what did it matter anyway? Immediately I had hugged her, she ran off to the kitchen, brought back a cloth and cleaned it up perfectly.

Like all mothers and daughters, we had had our conflicts. It was a necessary part of growing up for both of us. Understandably she had felt very angry when Corin and I got divorced; during her teenage years all these strong feelings came flooding out, and it was hard for me to find a way to console her.

She was extremely independent, very clever, and determined to be an actress. Never having had a real ambition in my life, I admired her commitment. Also I welcomed her blossoming beauty. I could never understand friends who resented their daughters' desirability and saw it as a threat. What on earth did they want? Some lump stomping around to reassure them that, Mirror, Mirror, on the wall, they were still the fairest in the land? You can't be Snow White for ever. Even she had to age, and maybe the handsome prince dumped her and went off with a bimbo. *Help!* Long Tall Sally's got fat, and has a drink problem. *'Où sont les neiges d'antan?'*

Like all mothers I dreaded the day when my pigeons would fly the coop. When Jemma and Luke were tiny I had of course bought *Sergeant Pepper* and that song, 'She's Leaving Home', did my head in. I would look at Luke crawling across the floor, and Jemma skipping, and anticipate the wrench to come. In Jemma's case, the wrench was hard: she was seventeen, and we had been to see the film *ET*. On the way back she informed me that she was moving out that very evening. I had no advance knowledge that could have prepared me. This was Jemma's way – no pleadings, no arguing, just a *fait accompli*. What a time to choose! We had both sobbed our way through *ET*; still fresh in our minds was the image of the little chap saying 'Home, home', his long finger pointing sadly at the sky, and we both found this parting of the ways very painful.

We cried as Jemma packed, and hugged and hugged, but it was clear that she needed to go. It is so important to let your children leave well; then they will always come back to you. When their need for freedom outweighs their need for home comforts, they must be given their head, and you must learn to face the future without the delights of a large family environment.

The main reason for Jemma's decision was her dislike of my then boyfriend. I knew he was not the sort of person she would have wanted me to live with, but foolishly I had not appreciated the depth of her antagonism. She wanted to go and share with her cousins Joely and Natasha at Vanessa's house in Chiswick, and I was happy about that because they had always been very close. Joely had once come to live with us while Vee was in New York starring in *Lady from the Sea*, and they always spent birthdays and sometimes Christmas together.

I recall one birthday of Tasha's: Vee had hired a cinema and shown *Camelot*. There is a scene at the end when Vanessa is to be burnt at the stake, and although the little girls could see perfectly well that Vee was sitting beside them, they cried so much that we had to take them out!

One cold Sunday morning in the mid seventies, when the children were still young, the phone rang: it was Tasha in a very distressed state. She explained that on the front page of the *Observer* there was a defamatory article about Corin and Vanessa; she didn't know where Vanessa was or what to do. I suggested that she and Joely should take a taxi to my home and that together we would sort something out. I lit the fire in the drawing room and organized a joint in the oven, thinking how pleasing and calming delicious smells from the kitchen and roaring log fires are.

I bought the *Observer* and the article was indeed defamatory: it implied that Corin and Vanessa's political activities included bullying and threatening behaviour towards people who did not agree with their views. I was shocked and did my best to track Corin down, but he was away.

Natasha and Joely duly arrived in tears, and by this time Jemma and Luke were also in a state. What on earth was I to do? I tried to change the subject, but to no avail. So I decided to take them to the Walt Disney cinema to see *One Hundred and One Dalmatians*. Well, the prospect did cheer them up immensely, though it filled me with gloom. How can you relate to Walt Disney when your husband (albeit estranged) has been attacked in vicious newspaper headlines? Still, we had lunch, and set off on our expedition.

The Walt Disney cinema, this haven of the nuclear family, is no place to visit when your family life is under stress. A veritable army of Mummys and Daddys and Peters and Janes are there to remind you what a mess you've made of your own life! Nostalgia prevailed. Strains of 'Some Day My Prince Will Come' came unbidden to my mind. 'Where did he get to anyway?' I thought crossly. For the first time I sympathized with the Ugly Sisters! This discovery came as a huge shock. I tried vainly to boost myself with a dose of cynicism: after all, just think of all the dramas that must lie behind the closed doors of these Happy Families. But the cosy, sentimental atmosphere was on their side. The children were happily engrossed in the film, but I was distracted by the sight of two large heads and two small ones repeated *ad infinitum* all over the cinema.

I was very relieved to be back in St Martin's Lane, where people were doing normal things like shouting at each other! The film had done the trick for the children, however, and as we went home for tea in a taxi I felt very protective of the four of them: I prayed they might all 'live happily ever after'.

Natasha and Joely had started on the boards earlier than Jemma, and were both enjoying great acclaim. But it was soon her turn: she was beautiful and intelligent, and had an anarchic wit. They have never competed with each other; rather, they have been mutually supportive – no sibling rivalry there. Recently, Jemma and her family flew out to New York for Natasha's wedding to Liam Neeson. When they arrived at their hotel, Tasha had not only filled their suite with flowers, but had thoughtfully provided nappies for the baby! Jemma, Tasha and Joely shared a hen night before the wedding.

Some years ago, after the death of Sir Michael Redgrave, a

memorial tribute at the Old Vic had been arranged by Vanessa and Corin. Many great luminaries of the theatre were there to perform in his honour. Luke and I sat in the darkened stalls, feeling extremely nervous. Jemma was still at drama school and was to perform a scene from *The Taming of the Shrew* (a part, I wickedly joked to her, that Shakespeare must have written with her in mind!). When her piece was announced, I whispered to Luke, 'Wouldn't you like to be performing on that stage tonight?'

'Mum,' he replied, 'I'd rather be knocked over by a bus!' and I agreed.

At the party afterwards, Dame Peggy Ashcroft came over and whisked Luke away. 'You shall be my escort for the evening,' she said. I too had always found Luke to be the perfect escort. He was much in demand.

After she left drama school, the first time I saw Jemma act was in Strindberg's *Easter* in Leicester. As I wandered through the city there were posters of her wherever I looked. I arrived at the theatre, feeling nervous, and there again were the posters, and her name writ large. To my astonishment, I burst into tears, a lump in my throat the size of an apple. Why? It was a mixture of pride, relief and love. The lump remained throughout the performance. I need not have been worried for her – she was excellent, and got wonderful reviews. She was on her way.

My chemotherapy course continued. For two weeks after a session I felt dreadful, but would always rally in the third week, feeling near to normal. They were damn clever, these doctors! If, during the third week, I had still felt lousy, the odds are that I would never have gone back for more; but, as with the pain of childbirth, the memory fades, and there you are again, ready to have another one. I must stress here that many people cope perfectly well with chemotherapy, and carry on as usual with their work and private lives. I have no wish to be a

29

scaremonger and alarm anyone else who might be facing treatment with this drug, but this is a record of my experience and the symptoms I felt.

During this time I had a weekly treat: the actor Jeremy Brett, our incisive Sherlock Holmes, heard about my condition and took me out for dinner. His second wife had died of cancer, and he understood, like no one else, what I was going through. He would book the same table at our favourite restaurant, and treat me like a princess. We had been friends for many years, and although the waiters treated us like a courting couple, our relationship was purely platonic. Nevertheless, it made me feel wonderful. I would take the trouble to dress up and put on make-up, and even after my hair had begun to fall out he would flatter me disgracefully. Jeremy must be one of the handsomest men ever, and one of the nicest, and I responded to his kindness like a parched plant does to water.

When I found out that I had cancer, I realized there could be no messing about in complicated affairs that might bring grief. Family and friends were what I needed, not the insecurity of an unstable relationship. That was something I could no longer afford. I was not involved with anyone when I got cancer, and resolved that if Prince Charming himself turned up (at last), I would run a mile.

My track record in that department had been appalling! I would meet some guy, and despite the dark and dire warnings of my friends that he was a womanizer, shit, bastard, con man, in I would go, oblivious of everything but *him*. I was like Titania in *A Midsummer Night's Dream*. Some mischievous sprite would sprinkle a magic potion on my eyelids, and there I was, blind as a bat to reality, until the day I awoke and found myself with Bottom, an ass's head on his shoulders! I exclude my ex-husband from this folly, and Jeffrey Bernard, though many would say that Jeffrey was the worst offender of all!

I have a cartoon on my wall which I cut out of a newspaper.

A mink-coated mother admonishes her daughter: 'He may be sexually attractive, Fiona,' goes the text, 'but he's socially unacceptable and financially repulsive!' My poor mother and I had acted out this scene over and over again! Now it was time for a change on every front.

On and on went the chemotherapy, and on and on went the balding process. A woman's hair, they say, is her crowning glory. I had always had long, thick, pre-Raphaelite hair, so wavy that when modelling in the sixties I had been obliged to iron it under brown paper for the Shrimpton look of the time. It had been a great triumph for Bob Champion to ride his brave horse twice over Beechers and go on to win the National, having won his fight over cancer. I couldn't help feeling that keeping my long red hair was just as important for me.

One morning I went to the bathroom and had a good look at my new self in the mirror. My hair was like that of a Victorian doll – bald patches with little tufts sprouting out here and there. My eyes were tiny and red like a rat's, another side effect. Tears started rolling down my cheeks as I surveyed this fearsome sight. How could I have come to this? How? Well I *had* come to this and I had to handle it. How dare I waste tears on myself? For heaven's sake, what was so special about me? I was not one of those people who think, 'Why me?' when they get cancer; I mean, why *not* me?

Hamlet says of his mother while looking at Yorick's skull, 'Now get you to my lady's chamber, and tell her, let her paint an inch thick, to this favour she must come.' All I was dealing with was the curse of vanity, and I had my share of that. 'Vanity, vanity, all is vanity', it says in Ecclesiastes, and it was time to divest myself of this folly. I simply had to forget that I had once been beautiful. Now I was ugly. So what? What difference did it really make in the great scheme of things? But then I remembered how the flattery and desire of men had always been a delight to me. It gave me a feeling of power, and I had basked in it. Well, I certainly would not be able to bask in it any more.

There is a marvellous passage in Sara Maitland's short story 'Rapunzel Revisited', which just about summed it up for me. After many years Rapunzel returns to her tower: 'So it is impossible for me to shape my future, although that is what I came to do. I have been the child, and the beloved and the queen and the widow. I have come to a place where I need a new story, a new way of seeing and I am so entangled in the old ones, unbrushed and unbraided, that I cannot let down my hair and haul up a future.' Priorities had to be changed and conceit had to go out of the window.

Ageing happens to all of us, but with chemotherapy it happens so quickly that you don't have a period of adjustment. Oh no! One day you are feeling pretty neat, and then *bang!*, to quote Martin Amis, you are ageing a year a month. In search of some good advice on ageing, I flicked through the pages of a chapter that Gabriella and I had compiled for our book. Various women had given us their tips on the problem. For example, Jean Shrimpton had said, 'I wrinkled early – so by now I am thoroughly used to my well of fine lines, and am not unduly bothered by them.' If someone as beautiful as Jean could be so pragmatic, then why shouldn't I be? From Lady Edith Foxwell: 'Always have the spirit of adventure. Never be false or become embittered, and never acknowledge when you're beat.' That sounded good. Jilly Cooper told us, 'I survive with a large vodka, the uncritical adoration of animals, and a potting shed where you can be alone and, when necessary, hide from the bailiffs.' Not having a garden, I could hardly have a potting shed, but the vodka was good advice; my place for hiding from the bailiffs was under my bed!

Jean Rook thought that Englishwomen age badly. They give up, while French women retain their sexuality until they drop dead on the Champs-Elysées. The best thing is not to give a damn, be comfortable with yourself, and keep your sense of humour. Well, it's hard to dredge up much humour when you've got little red rat's eyes, but I did my best. I simply learned to laugh at myself, and my previously held pretensions. A relief, really.

And then there was a book of poetry that Jemma had given me written by that great survivor, Maya Angelou. She had underlined one of the poems; she said that it reminded her of me. Here is the last stanza:

> Pretty women wonder where my secret lies.
> I'm not cute or built to suit a fashion model's size,
> But when I start to tell them,
> They think I'm telling lies.
> I say,
> 'It's in the reach of my arms,
> The span of my hips,
> The stride in my step,
> The curl of my lips
> I'm a woman
> Phenomenally,
> Phenomenal woman
> That's me.'

The fact that my daughter saw me as a phenomenal woman reduced me to tears. I *had* to live up to her faith in me.

The papers were full of women dying from cancer. Jill Ireland got the most coverage, but it appeared as if no one died of anything else. Then it happened to Jean Rook. She had been a wonderful friend, and it was hard to believe that such a strong, resourceful woman could be felled by this bloody disease. It was tragic, and it scared me a lot. She had been such a source of strength to me.

I was too ill on chemotherapy to make it to her memorial service, but my prayers were with her and her young son, Gresby, her pride and joy. After Jean's death, it was time for another reassessment. I realized that I was not only dealing with cancer, but with mid-life crisis as well.

When does this awareness of mid-life crisis start? Often it begins in small, innocuous ways. Suddenly you hear yourself yell at your teenage offspring, 'Turn down that terrible racket!' as alien sounds blast out of their rooms. You! You who used to curl your lip, talk tough, and dress like a tart because that's how Elvis and John Lennon liked their girls to look.

One evening you settle down to re-watch *The Graduate*, and are shocked to discover that you no longer identify with Katharine Ross. Now it is Mrs Robinson, once so scorned, who has your sympathy. How strange it all is.

One woman may rue the passing of her academic aspirations as she cooks the family lunch, while another, who had reached the peak of a rewarding career, yearns for the children she never had time for. Most of the options you once took for granted are no longer open to you. You will never be discovered, act at the National Theatre, or make it big in Hollywood. You did not get that degree you thought you'd fit in somewhere. You won't be writing that novel and winning the Booker Prize. You never did get rich, nor did you, nor will you ever, save the world!

Luckily I did not harbour a feeling of regret at this time in my life. I had two wonderful children, and had enjoyed a successful career as a costume designer for films and commercials. I had written two books which had had a small success both here and in America, and was now working on romantic fiction. It was real rubbish, but I enjoyed writing it. As to my future, I did not think of it. I had learned to live one day at a time. What else can you do when you are so ill?

One day when I was out shopping, thinking that I had covered my head in such a way as not to affright the multitudes, a youth started shouting at me, 'Hello, baldy!'

It was a sickening moment. As soon as I got home I knew

it was time to deal with the problem of my hair loss. I rang Wig Creations, a theatrical wig-makers which I had used when working as a costume designer. They explained to me that their wigs were made of real hair, difficult to manage and very expensive. They put me on to Hair Raisers, a wig company in Holborn which sold acrylic wigs.

A friend drove me to the West End as I was still too shaky on chemo to go there on my own. The staff were very helpful and I soon found the perfect thing: thick, long hair with a fringe just like my own had been. It didn't look like acrylic; in fact it looked quite natural. My friend burst into tears and hugged me. 'Oh, Deirdre,' she said, 'you look like yourself again.'

The trip had been a great success. Once more I had the confidence to venture out, and even thought I looked quite good despite my little red rat's eyes. Jemma had finished playing in *The Three Sisters* with Vanessa and Lynn and *Our Town* was soon to open in the West End. She wanted me to go to the first night, but I was still feeling wretchedly sick and was therefore worried that I might have to leave and cause a disturbance. She thoughtfully arranged for me to have a box.

Apart from the longing to see her performance, what woman could resist the thought of meeting Alan Alda, that tall, lanky, witty, handsome star of *M*A*S*H*. Alas, I didn't have the chance, typical of my luck! However, wearing my new wig and a new dress, I set off for the theatre with my great friend Robin Saikia feeling a million dollars. I had never imagined that I could feel that way again, ever. The performance started and Jemma was quite marvellous but, sure enough, the old symptoms of sickness and exhaustion took over and I went to sleep in the back of the box, missing half of the play. Nevertheless, I had made it there, and that made me feel I was coming alive again.

Then, all of a sudden, I began to go downhill fast. My exhaustion increased, and soon I found myself lying in bed all day. I could barely make it to the bathroom and back to bed. Because of the change in my taste buds, very common in chemo, I had taken to eating jam sandwiches, jellies and ice-cream – nursery food. But now a cup of tea was all I could manage.

Friends who visited me on a regular basis didn't notice my decline; to them it seemed gradual. I attributed it all to chemotherapy, and decided I would have to give it up. One day in the bathroom, as I clung on to the basin to keep myself upright, I looked in the mirror. The sight of my ashen, skull-like face was such a shock that I decided not to look at myself again. I didn't realize that I was dying.

Then fate took a hand. Jemma came to visit me with my dear friend Jennie Bark. Unbeknownst to me they both went into the kitchen where they started crying: they could see I was just about finished. They saved my life. Another twenty-four hours and I wouldn't be writing this book. They rushed me to the Marsden where they had booked an emergency bed. As I lay there in the ward, plugged into just about everything, a great feeling of peace enveloped me. I felt safe at last.

Jemma had rung round the family and close friends, thinking I might be dying, so I lay there drifting in and out of consciousness, while Corin and his wife Kika and many friends sat around my bed. I didn't have any idea how ill I was; I just thought they were so nice to come and see me. It was a warm and happy way to start my long stay in hospital.

But how desperately alone I felt the following morning, waking in an unfamiliar environment – alien sounds, tea trolleys rattling along, intrusive bright light, nurses with cheerful smiles bustling about; another country.

I lay back, fearful. Why was I here? Why had I been rushed

in? What was wrong with me? This certainly was not a side effect of chemotherapy; was I dying? Oh God, was I dying?

I noticed a bandage round my wrist. Had I tried to commit suicide? A tube came from under the bandage and I followed it upwards and saw that it was attached to a bag full of blood on a pole. What on earth was this? Nightmare images of Hieronymus Bosch began to flock into my mind. A cancer ward, full of the dead and dying. Oh, dear God, please help me to be strong. Please, *help me*.

A woman in the next bed leant towards me, saying, 'You look a different person this morning, dear. I was ever so worried about you last night.'

I didn't reply. I didn't want to hear anything she had to say. Or what anyone else had to say. I wanted only to isolate myself from my surroundings and pretend this wasn't happening. I decided then and there that I would discharge myself at once. They couldn't make me stay. I wanted to be home, in familiar surroundings. That was it. I would leave as soon as possible. Having come to that decision I felt better, so I sat up a little in order to inspect my surroundings.

There were about a dozen beds in the ward, occupied by women of all ages. A young woman sat on her bed holding a bag of urine attached to a long tube. A catheter. I wondered if it was temporary or permanent. She began to cry quietly and a nurse came over to comfort her. The scene upset me. I had no desire to see other people's pain – I had only just about learned to cope with my own! I lay back again, retreating into my own space. 'You don't have to look, you'll be going home in no time. Just keep yourself to yourself,' I thought. 'No need to get upset; just look at the ceiling and think about happy times and you'll emerge unscathed.'

Eventually a young doctor came over and sat on my bed. 'How are you feeling, Deirdre?' he asked. 'Don't worry now, you are going to be perfectly all right.'

'Well, can I go home then?' I asked him.

He looked at me and smiled. Slowly he shook his head. 'Of course you can't go home. You have been a very sick woman, but we got you in time. You were suffering from acute septicaemia, which means that your blood had been totally poisoned. We gave you several blood transfusions during the night, but you will need more, many more; you must have a very strong constitution to have survived that level of septicaemia.'

I was shocked. How could this have happened? The doctor answered my unspoken question.

'We will have to do more tests to find the true cause, but we suspect that it's connected with your coil. You see, when you are receiving chemotherapy your immune system breaks down, and small infections that are usually halted by your immune system become rampant.'

Well, this was news to me. Nobody had told me that my immune system might break down under chemotherapy, and it was not in any of the books or pamphlets that I had read on the subject. It was deplorable.

'I think, my dear,' he continued, 'that we are probably looking at a hysterectomy here. I am not sure yet, but I would like you to think about it in order to get used to the idea.'

A hysterectomy! I had had friends who had undergone this operation, the surgical removal of the uterus, and they had been tired for a long time after the operation, sometimes depressed. But after having cancer, acute septicaemia and all, this was no problem for me. A hysterectomy would be a tragedy for a young childless woman, but I had two children, and I had never shared the grief some women feel when they stop having periods. In one book about the menopause I had read this sad little piece: 'I still had some sanitary pads left and had been meaning to throw them out for some time, since I no longer needed them. I went to throw them out and then

I thought, "No, I'll keep them just in case." I stood there with them in my hand, not knowing what to do. Then I sat down on the bathroom floor and sobbed my heart out.'

Relinquishing a part of one's youth is always tricky – but periods? Surely that is a relief. They were always interfering with life: they stopped you playing tennis, swimming, riding, dancing, skiing; and, for my generation, there was the embarrassment factor. When buying Tampax as a young girl I would wait for hours to make sure that the assistant was female, and even then I would blush.

All this reminds me of a piece in *Portnoy's Complaint* when Portnoy's mother calls him to the bathroom door and tells him that he must go to the neighbourhood store to buy a packet of sanitary towels. Portnoy's response is that he would rather his mother bled to death on the bathroom floor than that he should have the appalling embarrassment of such an excursion! How pleasant to be free of all that hassle. I would have no regrets.

As the doctor left he said, 'You've seen the last of chemotherapy. It will be some time before you are strong enough for the operation, if it is necessary, so I think you should plan to be in here for some time while we build you up.'

The good news and the bad news: it was brilliant that I was not obliged to carry on with my chemotherapy course, but there was not to be a quick flight from the cancer ward. On balance, the good news won; it was up to me to adjust myself to my new, hopefully temporary, home.

3
Cancer Ward

Then on the shore
Of the wide world I stand alone, and think
Till love and fame to nothingness do sink.
– *John Keats*

I lay back on my hospital bed and tried to take it all in. There was so much to absorb. I had nearly died; had I felt close to death as some do? No, I couldn't really say that I had any out-of-body experience.

If Jemma and Jennie had not come to see me, would I have been dead today? With all my positive thinking, I had never really believed that I was so near death. I had fought them when they insisted on getting me to hospital – I was scared. But once there, I had felt relieved to be in the hands of professionals. A few days previously I had rung the Royal Marsden and asked an outpatient nurse whether it was normal to feel so weak. She had replied that I should come to Outpatients that afternoon. I explained to her that I would not be ringing if I felt strong enough to do that.

I felt stunned by the fact that you can be dying and yet have no warning bells. That you can just lie there and let it happen. How pathetic! No 'Do not go gentle into that good night . . . Rage, rage against the dying of the light' for me.

Anyway, here I was and here I would have to stay. It was one thing to be ill with cancer in the comforting environs of one's own home, leading a reasonably normal life, but here I was to be surrounded by it night and day, with no let-up. Outside you could forget about the dreaded illness for hours, for days, but not here. Here the bloody thing was always the topic, the *only* topic, and it felt claustrophobic. This, however, would be my new reality.

'Toughen up, buttercup', the saying goes. Just take it day by day and see how you get on. No previous convictions. No previous life. Just the here and now. Thinking along those lines was a help. I stopped avoiding my surroundings like the plague and decided to dive, head first, into this freezing unknown pool.

I was also beginning to understand the significance of the visits of family and friends the night before. They had come because they thought that perhaps I would not survive. They had all reacted in different ways, I heard later, and were all terribly shocked. My closest man friend, Robin Saikia, who was staying at my flat in order to take care of me, reacted the worst of all. He felt guilty that he had not spotted the warning signs – but how can you when you see someone every day? He had gone up to a nurse and asked her if I would survive the night. She was hopeful but unconvincing. Jemma had had to depart for the theatre, upset and worried, but relieved that I was now in good hands.

That first morning people arrived in droves, all so relieved that I'd made it through the night. Corin and Kika brought me some lingerie, Jennie brought me a bottle of scent, others brought books, flowers and plants so my bedside table soon began to look less clinical. I remembered Corin saying to me that he hated staying in hotels on foreign locations; he always took lots of books and photographs with him which he would strew untidily about the cold, unwelcoming room to make it feel like home. That was precisely what was happening to me, and very comforting it was too.

It was very strange learning to negotiate going to the bathroom taking my pole with me. I kept tripping over – much to the amusement of the other patients, who sailed around with theirs like swans.

The food was very reasonable, but it appeared at such odd hours: lunch at a quarter to twelve, tea at three, supper at a quarter to six, and cocoa at seven. I still had very little appetite, but I realized I had to force food down my throat – never a problem with me in the past, unfortunately! I have always espoused the 'eat, drink and be merry' philosophy; the alternative – living soberly on diets – would take so much joy out of life. I suspect my attitude had something to do with my Mediterranean upbringing. Friends would occasionally sneak in the odd bottle of wine; there is nothing I would have enjoyed more, but I decided I had to face this new experience without props. Without props, that is, except cigarettes. You just can't give up everything!

Nowadays there is a room for smokers in the Royal Marsden. This must sound very strange, but the consultants realize that in a life/death situation it is impossible to relinquish *all* your old habits, however bad. Indeed, if you are forced to do so, the stress you suffer is counter-productive. When I was there the hospital was being refurbished so there was no smoking room. As I grew stronger, and had learnt how to wander about attached to my pole, I roamed the corridors until at last I found an ashtray near a row of benches. I soon discovered that this was where the 'bad gang' hung out, and I joined them.

Sitting there, sipping tea from a mug and puffing away, I came across some fascinating people, fellow spirits who, despite their illness, had decided to be politically incorrect. One young man I met round the ashtray was a real Jack the Lad. He was in a wheelchair with his leg strapped out in front of him. He explained that he had cancer of the ankle. I asked him what kind of therapy they were giving him.

'I'm on the leeches, aren't I,' he replied. *Leeches!* Was he having me on? The last time I had heard of leeches was when, as a child, I read a story about Robin Hood, who had died in a convent from having too many leeches applied to his arrow wound. I had cried, and hated the nuns who had murdered my hero.

'Yeah, leeches,' he continued. 'They breed 'em here. They put 'em all over my ankle – disgusting, innit?' I could not but agree.

I asked a nurse if what Jack the Lad had said was true, and she explained that it was, that when leeches suck blood they secrete a healing substance into the patient's bloodstream. I was fascinated. It was reassuring to know that such an archaic form of treatment, in the midst of all the daunting implements of modern technology, was still useful.

For the next few days flowers, plants and cards kept on arriving; my cubicle began to look like a florist's shop and the ward ran out of vases. I received a huge tropical plant from Vanessa, with a loving card. I was very touched because, over the years, Vanessa, Corin and I had become estranged because of our differing political beliefs. But I had never stopped loving them, and now I knew that whatever our differences they still cared for me.

I had always remained in touch with my beloved mother-in-law, Rachel Kempson. She was upset when Corin and I found it necessary to part but now she was, as always, a source of strength, visiting frequently, full of optimism and love.

Lynn wrote to me in hospital from America, saying that she had lots of friends suffering from cancer who had made good recoveries. Because she lived in the States there had been scant communication between us. It felt comfortable to be back in the family group. I reflected how, so often, good things can come out of bad.

I began to feel embarrassed about the number of visits and flowers I was receiving. Some women in the ward never had any visitors and, although my flowers were spread around the ward for all to enjoy, I felt that the other patients must need their own testaments of love. When I became strong enough, I went and talked to them; my family and friends did likewise. I felt spoilt; nothing wrong with that, you may think, in the circumstances, but it was in the teeth of other people's loneliness and suffering. I was a very fortunate woman, and I never forgot it for a second. I decided there and then that when I was well again, I would become a visitor and help those who were lonely and afraid as I had been helped.

Jemma was remarkable. She came to see me every day. She was still starring in *Our Town* and I was concerned about her spending so much time with me, especially when she had a matinee. It was a very stressful time for her. '*Our Town*,' says Thornton Wilder, 'is an attempt to find a value above all price for the smallest events in our daily life.' One of Jemma's speeches is delivered after Emily (the character she played) has died. She is allowed back to visit her family one last time, and says through her tears:

> I didn't realize. So all that was going on and we never noticed. Take me back up the hill – to my grave. But first: Wait! One more look.
>   Goodbye, goodbye, world. Goodbye, Grovers Corners . . . Mama and Papa. Goodbye to clocks ticking . . . and Mama's sunflowers. And food and coffee. And new ironed dresses and hot baths . . . and sleeping and waking up. Oh, earth, you're too wonderful for anybody to realize you. Do any human beings ever realize life while they live it? – every, every minute?

It was very moving, and I know that her anxiety about me made it all the more poignant. Alan Alda was a tower of strength and would sometimes hug her in the wings when she couldn't hold back the tears. How strange it was that every night she spoke these lines, I was learning the truth of every day: that I must attempt to find a value above all price for the smallest events in my daily life.

Now, stuck in hospital, I cherished Jemma's daily visits. How I loved her. In a curious way, perhaps because of the strangeness of our surroundings (it was neither my place nor hers), we became closer than ever before. We talked about teenage trauma – things we had never before discussed, and discovered areas of each other which were fresh and new. Because I was so vulnerable and had no defences, she found it easy to relinquish hers, and it has paved the way for an easy relationship and mutual enjoyment. Recriminations were a thing of the past.

In contrast, I was sad when one or two of my close friends dropped me as if cancer were contagious. I had read about this syndrome, but was nevertheless hurt by it. They couldn't handle it, my friends said. Well, *why* couldn't they? *I* was the one doing the handling; I simply needed their support. The pain of this abandonment went very deep. Despite the continued presence of all my positive friends, I found, strangely, that you go on missing those who leave you. We had all shared in each other's crises, behaved well and behaved badly to each other; I had presumed that old friendships would stand the test of this harsh reality. But I was out in the cold now, and felt it, just because I had an unpleasant illness.

I suppose that some people are very simply afraid. I was astonished to hear Marjorie Proops admit, in an interview with Dr Anthony Clare on the programme *In the Psychiatrist's Chair*, that she was so terrified of death she could not bring herself to walk past an undertaker's. It was a very brave admission from a counsellor, and there must be millions like her.

One friend was suffering from clinical depression and

couldn't face the hospital. That I understood only too well. In my late twenties I had been severely depressed, and while cancer is a terrible illness, clinical depression is a living death, and I knew which I would choose.

I was adjusting quite well to my new world – the ward, the nurses, the sick, the dying; the shared happiness when a patient was discharged; the shared sorrow at bad news; the empathy with those constantly vomiting behind closed curtains as a result of chemotherapy. I was glad I was not in a private room. One day, while wandering about in my dressing gown, I inadvertently entered the private wing. The difference in atmosphere was palpable. I found myself in a large sitting room where several nervous-looking women, dressed up to the nines, were pretending to flick through *Vogue*. Some were even wearing hats. They looked at scruffy NHS me in surprise and I was glad to get out of there and back to my cosy ward. Here I was witness to courage and kindness, and there grew up a sense of camaraderie, of being members of the same club (a club that, like Groucho, I would have wished not to join!). The compassion shown by everyone – from consultant to cleaner – was transforming what could have been a terrifying experience into a life-enhancing one.

I had expected the medical staff to be kind, but I was surprised to find that the cleaning staff, tea ladies, newspaper vendors and library ladies all took time off for a chat and a laugh, all contributing to the well-being of the patients.

People make very quick friendships in hospital, both with staff and with patients and their families. There was a woman I remember in particular; she was one of the 'bad gang' and we met regularly round the ashtray. She was in her early forties, with a teenage family and a husband who adored her. It's strange being a member of the club: you ask questions and share confidences that would appear in appallingly bad taste under other circumstances. Anyway, she explained to me that she had no hope left; it was simply a matter of time. Being no longer uncomfortable with these kind of revelations, I felt compelled to ask her how she handled it. She was so calm – no tears, no panic, just total acceptance. That word again, how important it is: *acceptance* – rolling with the punches, going with the flow. She explained to me that she lived near the sea and that every day she would walk along the beach to a patch that she felt to be her very own place on the planet. Sitting there she would watch the endless movement of the sea and meditate. 'Death is simply a passage,' she would say. 'I have come to terms with the fact that it is my turn to move on.' She seemed totally at ease with her situation, and would laugh and joke with us.

Would I be able to laugh and joke? I wondered. It is one thing to be fighting cancer tooth and nail, denying death, but quite another to be told that you've lost the good fight, for definite. Do not pass Go, do not collect £200. *Finita la commèdia*.

I remembered an article I had read on the subject:

> . . . I resent cancer being treated like some moral crusade, as if the way patients respond to it carries moral weight. It is almost like blaming someone for having cancer. If you have to be strong, and fight to beat it, does that mean you were weak to develop it in the first place? And if you have to win, what does it say about you if you lose . . . ?

Yes, what indeed does it say about you if you lose?

I decided that while in hospital I would not wear my wig. I didn't have the energy to worry about what I looked like, not even for the handsome young doctors. This was me, now, and I must live with it. I remembered that Vanessa had shaved her head for her role in *Playing with Time*, a film about the

Holocaust. But with her beautiful bone structure, and a scarf wrapped round her head, she looked as lovely as ever. And look at Yul Brynner: he looked better without his hair. But no Yul I! I needed a frame for my broad Irish face. It should never be revealed like this in all its glory! Still, it was time for me to learn my place in the changing physical scheme of things, and bite the bullet.

However, there was one woman doctor who was extremely provocative. She would *click, clack* up and down the ward in her high heels, twirling around and tossing her long hair as she viewed us lowly folk with an ill-disguised air of superiority. She might just as well have been out pulling in a nightclub. She didn't really have anything to do with our ward, but in she would come, Ms Perfection, gloating and preening. Well, she got to me. 'You just wait till I get better, then you'll see,' I grumbled childishly to myself. God knows what sick satisfaction she got out of it, but I'm afraid I rose to her bait like a trout to the fly. I should have pitied her if this was the only way she could get her fun, but some primeval instinct got the better of me, and I silently raged at my impotence to have a go. One day I got so irritated that I determined that next time she came prancing in, I would put on my make-up and my wig so that I could toss my acrylic hair every bit as coquettishly as she. Common sense prevailed in the end, however; it was time for me to put away childish thoughts and grow up.

Then my personal 'bonfire of the vanities' was put even more sorely to the test. For many years I had been friends with the American group, the Manhattan Transfer. I loved their music and first met them in the seventies after a concert. Janice (who sings 'Chanson d'Amour') became a close friend – or as close as you can be when separated by the Atlantic. One year, on the last night of a tour I gave a huge party for them, made legendary by the fact that many of the band were still dancing at eleven o'clock the next morning, thereby missing their flight back to the States.

I had read in hospital that they were in London for a few days, but never dreamed they even knew I was ill; still less that with their tight schedule they would come and visit me. Well, come they did; not just Janice, as I might have expected, but all of them. I saw them enter the ward and look around for my cubicle. I dived straight under my pillow in fright. It was one thing for old friends and family to see me like this, but these were people I had only known in glamorous surroundings. If I had had any advance warning I could at least have worn a wig. I lay under the pillow like a vole in its hole, waiting for intruders to depart its territory.

A nurse patted my pillow. 'Come out, Deirdre,' she said. 'You have some friends to see you.'

'I know perfectly well I have friends out there,' I thought furiously. 'Why the hell do you think I'm under my pillow?' *Come out*? How embarrassing! Eventually I emerged sheepishly, trying for all the world to look as if this was my normal behaviour.

They were very taken aback at my appearance, so I was able to explain why I had hidden from them. I did feel foolish, but they put me at my ease and soon it was like old times. They really cared: you learn who your real friends are all the time. Jemma arrived and they left together to go and see her in *Our Town*. Jemma had known them since she was a child, but now *they* would be the ones in the audience. They told me they would pray for me, and once again the lesson was forced home: it doesn't matter what you look like; just be true to yourself.

The day for my hysterectomy was drawing nearer. My only concern was that after the operation, when my ovaries were sent to the laboratory, they might discover another malignancy. 'Then I'll be riddled with it,' I worried. The medical team did their best to reassure me – they were ninety-nine per cent sure that nothing would be found, but it was one hell of a one per cent to think about.

A very nice woman came to occupy the bed next to me. She was to have a hysterectomy on the same day as me. She summoned a nurse over, and in a voice that could be heard in Hong Kong enquired, 'Do many people die while undergoing this operation?'

It was her use of the word 'many', as opposed to 'any', that got me. The nurse reassured her that nobody died of it, but the damage was done. The fragile barrier between stoicism and fear that prevailed in the ward had been broken, and we all began to look as petrified as she did.

I looked at the pile of books my neighbour had brought in with her. They were all about Death, and the Other Side. I tried my best not to take them as an Omen, but they all looked too much like an ill wind that would blow no one any good at all.

A nurse asked me if I would like to visit the intensive care unit in order to familiarize myself with it. Perish the thought! The sight of those places, even in films, with some poor sod's heartbeat pulsing across the screen, had nearly given me a heart attack. 'I'll handle it better semi-conscious,' I thought.

The night before my operation I received a phone call from Vanessa saying that her thoughts were with me. And then, treat of all treats, Luke managed to get through from Texas. It was so wonderful to hear his voice and know that he was safe. Although I missed him terribly, I was glad Luke had not been here when the crisis struck. His reaction to the news that I had cancer was to try and pretend it wasn't happening: he visited me less frequently, and when my hair began to fall out he was so devastated that we mostly communicated on the phone. He had always been very proud of me and how I looked, and he couldn't bear what was happening. It was far better for him to be abroad in pastures new. While Luke was away reverse charge calls would home in from all over the world, which resulted in a £1,000 telephone bill! I felt it was cheap at the price to be assured that he was well and happy, although British Telecom were not amused when it took me a year to pay it back!

On my return to the ward, Adam, the young doctor in charge of my case, came to see me. He told me the operation had been a great success and he was confident there was no malignancy. However, I would have to wait a few days for the lab report. I lay there, weak and in pain, trying not to worry about this, and kept it quiet from family and friends, who all assumed the worst was over.

It was my secret terror. I searched the faces of the nurses for any sign that they *knew something*. A pitying glance would have spoken volumes. It was rather like being on a bumpy flight: you keep your eyes glued to the air hostess for any sign of fear. I read my positive books with an unhealthy fervour. I listened and listened to Luke's meditation tape.

Then I became obsessed with the idea of swimming with dolphins. That was all I wanted to do – no longer was it my aim in life to marry Daniel Day-Lewis, or to look like Claudia Schiffer; just to swim with dolphins who would cure me, being the magical creatures they are. I would drift off in my mind to a turquoise sea where I would play with the dolphins, and we would communicate love and compassion. Looking back on it, a much easier option than marrying Daniel Day-Lewis! But the terror remained.

Would death simply be a passage to a better place? Books by Michael Bentine said so. I tried my best to believe that, but fear of the unknown kept vying with my inner wisdom, and these bouts of conflict always ended inconclusively.

Fear of the unknown . . . I'm an old Capricorn, and hate change of any sort, and I was looking at the biggest change known to man. OK, I'd nearly copped it once already, but then, I didn't know I was copping it. That's one hell of a difference. Now I would know that I was copping it. Could I be like my friend round the ashtray? I doubted it. I lay there, wrestling over and over with the possibility that I might soon be extinct, perchance to dream.

Socrates, while awaiting the hemlock, uttered the amazing words: 'I am not very likely to persuade other men that I do not regard my present situation as a misfortune, if I cannot even persuade you that I am no worse off now than at any other time in my life.' *How could he say that?*

> Will you not allow that I have as much of the spirit of prophecy in me as the swans?
> For they, when they perceive that they must die, having sung all their life long, do then sing more lustily than ever, rejoicing in the thoughts that they are about to go away to the god whose ministers they are. But men, because they are themselves afraid of death, slanderously affirm of the swans that they sing a lament at the last . . .

How to sing at the last? *What* to sing at the last? Well, certainly not 'Blue Suede Shoes'! Nothing mawkish like 'The Party's Over' or 'Send in the Clowns' (Jeffrey Bernard's favourite song). No, back to the Requiem Mass. 'The trumpet shall sound and the dead shall be raised, be raised incorruptible.' All too monumental – you can't feel cosy with that stuff. 'And did those feet . . .'? No! What about 'I danced in the morning when the world was begun, and I danced in the moon and the stars and the sun, and I came down from heaven and I danced on the earth; at Bethlehem I had my birth'? Joyful and accessible.

And then the conflict was resolved.

Adam came tearing down the ward, throwing his arms in the air like Gazza after a goal. 'Deirdre, Deirdre, you're going to be all right, your results are clear!' As he sat on my bed and held my hand, my eyes were moist. Despite his many patients and a huge workload, he had taken the time out to tell me himself, and seemed to feel joy at the result as intensely as I did. I wanted to hug him, but I just lay back, tears pouring down my cheeks; for a moment I relinquished my need to be strong at all times.

Who were these people – these dedicated people who worked night and day for others with scant financial reward, who shared your worries and joys, who gave of themselves so much? Who cleaned and comforted the incontinent, held and soothed those suffering from vomiting attacks, who smiled in the face of so much pressure, who cherished the dying? And they were so young. What awesome responsibility they held, and yet they were always cheerful, with kind words for everyone. I felt very ashamed of my fear of the cancer ward and seeing people dying; these people dealt with it all the time, with humanity and courage. I determined to learn from them.

And then there was Staff Nurse Trubshaw. We liked each other at first sight, and it was as if she had elected to be my personal nurse. She took on the most unpleasant tasks like giving me enemas and colonic irrigation. But for her kindness, I would have found these curatives an impossible intrusion. This book is in part dedicated to her, for I have never known anyone so selfless.

Liz Trubshaw was very pretty, with a bubbly, humorous personality. She worked so hard, and I knew that often after a long, exhausting shift, she would return home to study for her exams. Her work was everything, and she told me how she felt rewarded when patients got better. She also told me that when there was bad news for a patient, she and the other nurses would go to the staff room and cry, making sure that the patients didn't see or suspect anything.

She got on very well with Jemma, who organized for her and her boyfriend to go and see *Our Town*. After I left the Marsden, she would sometimes come and stay as I lived so close to the hospital – it saved her from trekking all the way to the other side of London, where she lived. On those occasions I felt so pleased to be doing something for her for a change. I understand she has now gone to Australia to get married and my gratitude will follow her all my life.

But there was one nurse who was a cow. Unfortunately, she took charge of our ward every night, and I dreaded her coming. After the hysterectomy I was in considerable pain. My painkillers were usually administered four-hourly, but sometimes at night the pain was hard to bear and I would push my button to request the pills. The nurse would saunter slowly over to my bed, look at her watch, and say, 'You have another five minutes before I can give you any more painkillers,' and with an unpleasant smile she would disappear from the ward for half an hour. Watch out! There's one on every ward.

We all have friends who suffer, or who have suffered, from serious diseases; it might be cancer, motor neurone disease, MS, Parkinson's . . . the list goes on. At times we may have thought that we could understand and sympathize with their suffering simply by virtue of being close to them. But when we ourselves are suddenly thrown into the dark abyss of serious illness, we soon begin to regard our friends in a new light. This is really a message for those who have never been really ill: it is very easy to become impatient, or exasperated, with an ill friend or relation, but you must remember that he or she is deploying a lot more bravery, beneath a cheerful front, than you may immediately realize.

One of my dearest friends, Penny Gordon, had had multiple sclerosis for twenty years. As I lay in my hospital bed I thought about her courage and realized that, however bad things might be now, one day I would walk out of the ward; she would never walk again. *How could I feel sorry for myself?*

Another seriously ill friend who was a great support to me was the actress Pippa Steele, married to writer Richard Whittington. She had had cancer for many years; when she first told me of it, I marvelled at her composure, never dreaming that one day I would find myself in the same boat. Despite the fact that she herself was in a very bad way, she would ring me with advice on how to cope with chemotherapy. Eventually she decided to give up the treatment: it was only spoiling what life she had left. She was facing certain death with a calmness that inspired all those who knew her. Her generosity of spirit, her wisdom and courage helped me in my determination to get on with my life in the way she had. She accepted death with grace and dignity, and I hoped that, if it came to it, I would do the same. I was very lucky to have such brave friends to help me through my crisis, and the debt I owe them is immeasurable.

When Jemma realized that I would be in hospital for some time, she decided to redecorate my flat as a home-coming present. It certainly needed it, but it was amazing of her to take on such a costly and time-consuming endeavour. She and my friend Jennie Bark, who was an interior designer, worked out what needed to be done, Jemma buying the new carpets, paint and lamps, Jennie doing the decorating, helped by friends.

I guessed something was going on, but it was Robin who revealed the extent of it. He arrived one evening in a state of great agitation. 'Your flat is full of mad women all the time,' he grumbled. 'They never stop shouting at me and I'm scared of them all. If Captain [my cat] shits on the floor, it's my fault. If I move a J-cloth one inch they fly into paroxysms of rage. "Where's my bloody J-cloth?" they scream at me. "I left it on the table especially so I could use it this morning. How could you do such a thing?"' Robin explained that this was all very new to him. He was used to people shouting at him, but what was so special about a J-cloth? 'And furthermore,' he said, 'they have decided to get rid of Captain.'

I adored my cat, but I could understand that, as Jemma was investing a lot of time and money in new carpets and a new sofa, the cat would have to go. Captain was a fine large animal, but he had very bad habits like peeing and shitting everywhere but in the appointed tray. He was removed by the Cats Protection League to a new home in the country. I miss him very much and wonder if cats have a memory and if he hates me for sending him away. I rang the Cats Protection League to find out where he was so that I might visit him, but their lips were sealed as tightly as those of a priest in the confessional.

A few days before I was due to leave the hospital, a young woman arrived and was put into the bed opposite mine. She was only twenty-one and so pretty. She wept and wept inconsolably and a nurse explained to me that she had undergone one course of chemotherapy, during which she had, of course, lost all her thick dark hair. Now she was due to start another course and could not face the prospect of being bald again. For the first time in hospital I got out my wig and put it on. She was amazed at the transformation. I gave her the number of Hair Raisers and she was greatly heartened. Sadly I heard later from a tearful Nurse Trubshaw that she had died.

The day dawned when I was to go home. I was still very fragile, but on the plus side I had lost a lot of weight. I dressed, put on my make-up and wig, and said goodbye to the many friends I had made. The young doctor, Adam, didn't recognize me, which was very pleasing, and I departed with mixed emotions. How marvellous the staff had been – I had learnt so much from their caring and kindness; and how brave the patients! The Marsden seemed to have the healing spirit infused in its walls. I knew I would miss it in many ways.

I visited the chapel before I left and said prayers of gratitude. It is quite beautiful, with lovely stained-glass windows, and fine paintings and sculpture. There is a notice board where patients write messages asking God to help them. One read, 'Dear God, please help me through this agony, I must try to be strong for my family, but sometimes I can't.'

As I left I thought of those still fighting their battle, and once again resolved that as soon as I was well enough, I would become a counsellor and help those who, unlike myself, did not have the support of family and friends.

My nervousness at being out in the real world once more was cut short by the complete transformation of my home. The drawing room had been carpeted and there was a new sofa, given to Jemma by Alan Alda as a farewell present at the close of their play. Paintings and mirrors had been rearranged, and there was a profusion of new plants and bowls of flowers. My bedroom had been completely done over: previously merely functional, it was now a French country cottage bedroom. Cream lace curtains hung at the windows, an antique patchwork quilt lay on the bed, and Jennie had stencilled roses round the walls. When I saw the kitchen and bathroom I felt I should immediately get *Homes & Gardens* to come and photograph them. I was enchanted. I had left a comfortable tip and had returned to elegance.

Friends arrived throughout the day bearing bottles of champagne, but I quickly grew tired. I snuggled down in my fine new bedroom filled with gratitude.

I knew that as soon as I was strong enough I would have to go back to the Marsden for a stint of radiotherapy. The malignancy was weakened, but had not disappeared. I could still feel the lump, this horrible intruder, but I would not dwell on it.

I had to muster all my strength for the battle to come.

4
Radiotherapy, Plastic Surgery and Bereavement

The thought of suicide is a great source of comfort: with it a calm passage is to be made across many a night. – *Friedrich Nietzsche*

The days passed by pleasantly enough. Friends were still coming round to cook meals and this, along with the pleasure at being in my transformed home, contributed to my well-being. I was still very tired, of course – that was to be expected – but the dire effects that I had been warned I would suffer after a hysterectomy – depression, loss of self-confidence and, later, loss of libido, simply did not occur. I was very fortunate in that respect.

I rested a lot, ate healthily, in fact did everything the doctors had advised in order to be fit for radiotherapy, which was due to commence in three months' time.

Three months felt like a long time, time in which to recharge my batteries, and they certainly needed recharging on all fronts. I had had a real bashing over the past nine months, both physically and mentally, and now it was time to take life easy, to indulge myself and just loaf about reading, with outings to restaurants; and to take stock for the first time of what had happened to me. Things had moved so quickly that it had been a case of just hanging in there; now I had time to reflect.

The mental exhaustion reminded me of a time in the late sixties when I had arrived at my psychiatrist's in a state of total confusion. 'I have different philosophies hurled at me all the time,' I said. 'My feminist friends tell me that the Workers Revolutionary Party is a seriously sexist set-up; my husband tells me that feminists are evasionists; and the Underground [*Oz* and *International Times*, and that lot] say that both the former groups are seriously boring. They are all ranting at me, all the time, and I don't know what to think any more.'

The doctor looked at me and smiled. 'I am going to order you to do something,' he said. 'This is not a suggestion, this is what you *must* do till I see you in a fortnight. You may only read women's magazines, nothing else – not even a newspaper – and we'll see what result that has.' I was outraged, how *dare* he patronize me like that? I glared at him. 'I am not insulting your intelligence, my dear,' he went on. 'It's just that your brain needs a rest.'

Now it was time to take his good advice once again. All of us need to take a complete rest sometimes, and that means not taxing the old brain cells either. I did exactly as he had suggested, and what a relief it was! I didn't exactly take up macramé or knitting, but I certainly cooked a few good meals!

The autumn of 1991 was cold, and I was looking forward to spending Christmas in the New Forest with my brother Patrick – watching the snow falling on meadows instead of into dirty London gutters and, if I felt strong enough, enjoying walks in the frosty countryside with the dog, and dozing by roaring log fires. Luke was still travelling round the world, but Jemma and her barrister fiancé, Tim Owen, and friend Robin were all to travel down together: a real family Christmas.

But then Patrick rang to tell me that our brother Robert had committed suicide by jumping off a fire escape at St Mary Abbot's Hospital, where he was being treated for schizophrenia.

Our beloved younger brother Robert. I went numb . . . I

couldn't cry like Patrick. For so long I had been bottling up my feelings in order to confront cancer and life in the Marsden that I had forgotten how to experience sorrow and grief. My emotional outlet there had been laughter, not tears. 'Always Look on the Bright Side of Life'! How hollow that rang.

He hadn't been messing around, had he? No cry for help from him – no, he had had enough and he simply put an end to it all. I admired his courage. No easy way for him: no comforting bottle of valium, no gas oven or car exhaust. He had walked up a fire escape and jumped. What had been going on in his mind? Perhaps he just threw himself into the blue sky, not caring about hitting the ground. The question haunted me then; it still does.

Think positive, think positive: he is at peace now – but where? In the bosom of the Lord? Where was the Lord when he was suffering so acutely from this foul illness? For a time my sorrow and anger made me lose sight of the strides that I had made in turning pain into a stepping stone to a new spiritual horizon. But although I momentarily lost sight of my new resolve, it was comforting to find out that the efforts I had made to be strong did not evaporate at the first testing crisis. I was able to handle the pain of bereavement. Would I have been able to a few years back?

Corin came round the minute he heard the news. Rob had lived in our flat in Coleherne Court for many years and Corin was a great influence on him, supporting him in his bid to go to university in America, where he obtained a degree in anthropology. (Our parents wanted him to take a degree in business studies and pursue a career in the City.)

Rob called himself Rob Hill, dropping the 'Hamilton' because he hated the upper-class connotations of a double-barrelled surname. He hated any form of hypocrisy or cant. 'I always felt that Rob was too sensitive, too gentle for this world,' Corin said as he tried to comfort me. 'A violent death for such a gentle man,' I thought bitterly.

Rob had begun to behave oddly in the early seventies. It was a very bad time for manifesting symptoms of schizophrenia because nobody really paid much attention to odd behaviour in those days. It was almost *de rigueur* and was known as 'doing your own thing'. Some of our friends had disappeared to India in search of dope and gurus, some to Glastonbury in search of the Holy Grail, and some to Ladbroke Grove in search of various substances and Heavy Metal sex.

My knowledge of schizophrenia then was confined to *Dr Jekyll and Mr Hyde* and from leafing through *The Divided Self* by R. D. Laing, who was required reading if you were to hold your own at trendy dinner parties. Little did I comprehend the complexities of this terrible illness. 'Schizophrenia: any of a group of psychotic disorders characterized by progressive deterioration of the personality, withdrawal from reality, hallucinations, delusions, social apathy, emotional instability, etc.' it says in the dictionary, and that sounds about right to me. Horribly right.

First, Rob developed religious mania, gave up all his worldly goods and became a tramp. For a while he dossed around in Chelsea and Kensington so I was able to keep an eye on him. Then he simply disappeared. Frantic with worry, I contacted the Salvation Army who are so brilliant at finding lost souls, but they failed to come up with anything. Our parents were dead, Patrick was living in Brazil, so I was left with the burden of responsibility for Rob. I was working very hard at this time, and was also taking care of two young children, and there was not much I could do but pray that he might appear soon.

Then, about a year later, a friend sent me a cutting from an Ilford paper: 'Vagrant Robert Lloyd Hamilton-Hill has been arrested rooting through dustbins; he has been taken into custody for delousing and psychiatric tests.' I had found him! He refused to come home but at least I knew where he was.

After some time I was able to get him under section to St Mary Abbot's Hospital, where they treated him with drugs. He slowly became his old self again and described his suffering to me. I had a glimpse of the terror he had lived in: he was convinced he was wicked and feared eternal damnation, punishing himself in an effort to save his soul.

Eventually he was well enough to move into a flat provided by MIND. He got a job, went again to the theatre and opera, and fell in love. In 1990 he married his beloved Shirley, an old friend of mine, and the future looked wonderful. But all the love in the world could not help him when the great bouts of darkness struck. He returned to hospital.

He came to visit me one day and told me a story I found very touching. That morning a man in the dormitory had deliberately left his bed unmade and had written a notice which read: 'This bed is left unmade as my protest against the continuing imprisonment of Nelson Mandela.' (Perhaps if it had been Winnie he'd have made it perfectly!) How remarkable that this man, under section in a psychiatric ward, could maintain such a high degree of dignity and integrity.

Shirley and Rob came to visit me a few days before he killed himself. He was in great spirits, witty, intelligent, full of joy and hope for the future. Now he was dead.

He loved the writings of H. D. Thoreau, so here is a quote in memory of him:

> I wanted to live deep and suck out all the marrow of life . . . to drive life into a corner and reduce it to its lowest terms, and, if it proved to be mean, why then to get the whole and genuine meanness of it, and publish its meanness to the world; or if it were sublime, to know it by experience, and to be able to give a true account of it in my next excursion.

I had observed many grieving families in the Marsden; now I had to deal with bereavement myself. My parents had died some ten years before. Although I missed them terribly, it was, I felt, part of the pattern of life. You expect that your parents will die before you. But the loss of a sibling – or worse, a child – simply does not fit in with the natural order of things. We are not able to console ourselves with the reassuring sentiments we feel on the death of a parent or grandparent who led a full and happy life. Instead, we feel robbed and cheated, especially when the death is so cruel and violent.

I found that the only way to console myself was to concentrate exclusively on the joyous times – and there were many which Rob, Patrick and I had shared over the years. I began to realize that this too was a form of visualization. It was yet another way in which my fight against cancer had strengthened me and enabled me to deal with other major crises in my life which formerly would have devastated me beyond belief. We must all remember that we have a core of strength within us, which is there to draw on in times of need.

During that bleak midwinter I was numb in heart, but with the arrival of spring my spirits lifted once more. I had regained some strength and was considered well enough to start radiotherapy, the treatment that uses high-energy rays to kill the cancer cells.

I had heard from friends who had undergone radiotherapy that the only real side effect was tiredness. I wouldn't be sick and I would get to keep my hair. It didn't sound too bad at all.

I must stress at this point that radiotherapy does not necessarily follow chemotherapy. It is quite usual to have one without the other. It is a decision taken by the specialist, who will do his or her best to suit your particular needs.

At the Marsden they explained to me that my treatment would last for three weeks and take place every day, Monday to Friday. I was very fortunate to live a mere ten-minute walk from the hospital, and I arranged for my treatment to take place at nine-thirty in the morning so that the rest of my day was free.

My first visit to the radiotherapy department involved going under the 'simulator'. This is a machine that takes X-ray pictures of the area to be treated to ensure absolute accuracy. I walked into a small white room, at the centre of which was a huge gantry holding the machine that would take the X-rays. Beneath it was a bed. It looked cold and sterile and very high-tech, and I felt lost and nervous. 'Come back, leeches,' I thought, 'all is forgiven!'

My doctor came in and was very understanding. She made me laugh as she drew line after line on my chest, breast, shoulder and neck, and I began to relax in the hostile environment. She explained to me that on no account must I wash the 'mapped' area or under my left armpit. 'Don't worry,' she reassured me, 'your sweat glands will cease to function when we start treatment.'

Phew, what a relief! I was still wearing a wig and the left side of my body looked like a map of the London Underground: no nice low-cut spring dresses for me – and if I were to be sweaty to boot, I would have really felt like a pariah.

The following day I started the treatment. I decided to use my visualization technique once again, both as a complementary therapy and to make the treatment more bearable. I resolved that the Marsden would be Oz, the great machine would be the Wizard who was going to cure me, and every morning, as I set off on my Yellow Brick Road, the streets of Chelsea seemed paved with gold.

As I walked along I concentrated on the healing powers of the world. I imagined that everything, the trees, the clouds, the flowers, were beaming great rays of healing into my cancer.

The radiotherapy room was identical to the simulator room, cold and clinical. Four nurses adjusted the machine. I had four areas to be treated and the map on my body helped them to site the ray correctly. When they had finished they would all leave the room, and I lay there alone, as still as I could. A buzz would then sound which meant the ray had been switched on. I visualized it as a beam of golden light in which was written the word 'healing'. I saw it coming closer and closer to my dark lump, transforming it into white stars, which in turn became wisps of cloud that floated up to the ceiling. I found using visualization enormously helpful. It certainly kept any feelings of loneliness and fear at bay.

As my treatment took place at the same time each morning I got to know other people who were booked in then. One woman told me that she had a journey of an hour and a half to get to the Marsden; after her five minutes of treatment she would drive an hour and a half to get home again. I noticed that as her treatment continued she became very tired and could no longer drive herself. She came to rely on members of her family, which must have been stressful for her. I was certainly fortunate to live so close.

One morning a young man of about twenty came in for radiotherapy. He had a friend with him, and looked extremely nervous. The friend accompanied him for the first few days but soon his terror evaporated and he felt able to come on his own, which says a lot for the staff who were able to put him at his ease so quickly.

I soon found out myself what it was like to become reliant on others. As the days went by the tiredness turned to exhaustion: it became difficult to do anything other than make it to the hospital and back. I must urge those who might be facing radiotherapy not to be worried by my experience; after all, I had just undergone chemotherapy and a hysterectomy – enough to floor anybody.

The side of my body that was being treated started to go red. I had been warned that this might happen, particularly as

I am the red-haired, freckled type who burns easily in the sun. The red patch covered my left breast and shoulder, went up my neck and round my back. It didn't hurt but it was unsightly – but then my whole body was pretty scarred and unsightly so I just remembered my 'bonfire of the vanities' and shrugged it off. My hair was beginning to grow back but I now looked like a convict so I stuck to my wig. I had had time to come to terms with my changed appearance, and I felt sorry for people who had to confront it suddenly, after a car crash or a fire, for instance.

Then I was faced by something that I had not anticipated. My left breast began to alter in shape and texture. It drew itself up and became firm and hard. Jane Fonda would have paid a fortune for it! The other one, alas, stayed exactly where it had been, hanging down, so no more getting away with not wearing a bra! I also had a hernia in my stomach so I had these three lumps, placed apparently at random across my chest! Think positive! Think positive!

I had waited for two years to have my hernia fixed on the NHS, and the week I was due to be operated on was the week I discovered I had cancer. The specialist at the Marsden advised me against having the operation then because I must save my strength for the more important battle. Not that I cared. The hernia had faded into insignificance.

On the last day of my radiotherapy course I discussed the problem of my non-matching breasts with the doctor, and she assured me that as soon as I had recovered from the treatment I could have plastic surgery at the Marsden to re-align them if I wished; wish I certainly did.

I had been warned that in some cases the tiredness actually increases after the end of therapy, and indeed I found that weariness suffused everything I did. It was not merely physical; I was totally unable to concentrate on reading or even watching television. This worried me, so I rang my doctor who explained that my whole system was suffering from exhaustion; it had simply broken down. She advised me to rest as much as I could – well, there was no hope of my doing anything else! – not to attempt to read and essentially just to loaf about. After all, as James Thurber puts it, 'It is better to have loafed and lost than never to have loafed at all!'

This was not as boring as you might imagine. I daydreamed the time away. My main fantasy was that I would make lots of money writing Mills and Boons. Thinking up plots for romantic fiction proved quite absorbing and the time passed quickly and agreeably. Week in, week out, I fell in love with my appalling macho heroes and was reminded of a quote by Dinah Livingstone: 'I don't understand those women who demand disgust in outraged arguments against penetration, make daisy chains to deck a sister's correct political gestures, who tick me off for craving impossible men.'

Thanks to the nurturing of family and friends, I slowly began to get stronger. The red stain on my left side faded, and life returned to normal. I was to have a biopsy in a few months' time, and the hospital staff seemed pleased with my progress. Spring changed to summer. I found the heat a problem because wearing a wig is very uncomfortable when the temperature is sky high. Still, I was not ready to go without it; it had become symbolic to me of my pre-cancer self, and I did not discard it until my hair had grown quite long.

To my great joy, Luke returned from his round-the-world trip. He looked emaciated, but was well enough. I cried when I saw him. Understandably it took him a while to orientate himself. His travels had changed his perception and vision of the world, and I thanked God that I was still here to see him again.

He had returned in time for Jemma and Tim's wedding, which was to be held in June. I liked and respected Tim enormously, as did Corin, and it had been a comfort to me when I was in the Marsden to know that, if things went wrong, Jemma had a good man to take care of her.

The ceremony was to take place at Chelsea Registry Office so Vanessa, Corin, Kika, Luke and I duly arrived early at Rachel's Chelsea home, where Jemma was getting dressed. There was the typical pre-nuptial panic when it was discovered that Jemma's circlet of fresh flowers had not arrived. This problem was solved by the hairdresser, who improvised from the bowls of flowers in Rachel's house. When at last Jemma emerged she looked stunning in her full-length cream lace dress. It was a moment of great happiness and pride for me, especially as I had feared that I might be too weak to attend.

The reception was held in a charming French restaurant owned by a friend of Jemma and Tim's, who had filled the three floors with flowers. The food was superb, the champagne flowed and the atmosphere was heady.

At one point the photographer took a picture of Jemma and her two cousins, Natasha and Joely. As I looked at those three young women, all beautiful, talented and, more importantly, so nice, I thought back to when they were children, remembering their growing pains, the happy times we had all spent together at Rachel's country cottage, their shared confusion over the Workers Revolutionary Party's role in their lives. I thought back also to the break-up of my marriage to Corin, and to the ideological conflict between him, Vanessa and myself. Now, as we all beamed and hugged each other, any discordant memories were forgotten. There was none of that frightening residual bitterness that, alas, so often lurks beneath happy smiles at functions like weddings. I have never understood those people who cling on to their acrimony as if their life depended on it.

*   *   *

The summer drifted along pleasantly enough, and I was gaining strength all the time. My energy level was building up, and soon I was able to go out shopping or for walks – all the things that normal people do. At long last the day dawned when I was to go back into the Marsden for plastic surgery on my right breast. I felt no nervousness about returning to the hospital where I had witnessed so much suffering. I knew that the Marsden's healing spirit would be there to strengthen me if I needed it. However, I did feel a little guilty that I was going there for plastic surgery – but I learned that the cancer consultants and doctors take one's desire to look and feel good again very seriously: plastic surgery is all part of treating the illness.

I duly arrived at nine o'clock with my suitcase, expecting to be in for a week. I was met by a very flustered young doctor who explained to me that they had had an influx of women needing cancer surgery and that these had priority over people like me. 'We tried to ring you,' he said, 'but we couldn't get through. We didn't want you to have this wasted journey.'

I told him that my phone had recently been cut off because I could not afford to pay the bill and we both started laughing. Honestly, what a thing to happen! My health might be improving but my finances were, as always, in a quagmire.

I had had many a run-in over the years with Messrs Gas, Electricity, Water Rates, BT and TV Licence. They menaced me like dragons. My TV sets had been removed on a regular basis, and I would have to walk miles out of my way to avoid the corner-shop man who had, oh so kindly, let me run up a bill that would have embarrassed Wall Street.

Still, living on the edge means you have to keep your wits about you, but being without a phone was always horrid. Like many women I can happily chat away all day on the thing, and living in a fourth-floor flat I felt cut off from life, like an eagle in its eyrie. When you phone people from call boxes all the time it costs a fortune. You put your money in, say, 'Hello, how are you?' and the pips go and you've got no more change. One day a funny thing happened: I was in a call box chatting away when I noticed a young man waiting. I had just put my head out of the box to tell him I would not be long when he said, 'It's all right, love, I've just got to put some of these up.' And, without more ado, he pushed into the box and stuck up advertising cards for vice girls. I was quite astonished. I mean, what a cheek!

My phone was still cut off when I arrived at the Marsden, with some trepidation, a few weeks later, but this time all was well. Jemma and Luke accompanied me, and the sympathetic staff nurse said that Jemma could take us out to lunch beforehand. This time it was wonderful to have Luke there too. I thought how things like having no phone mattered not at all when I had this happiness.

Once again, the sense of warmth and love I always experience in the Marsden enveloped me. I still felt a little guilty that I was only there for plastic surgery when I was surrounded by women who were ill but, as always, we all became friends and swapped stories. One case was very upsetting. In the bed opposite mine was a young woman in her mid twenties. She had secondary cancer and was naturally very worried. She was engaged to be married to a charming young man, who came to visit her every day. One morning she had a visit from her consultant and, as I looked at the closed white curtains round her bed, I prayed that the news would be good. He stayed for a long time, and then I heard her crying. 'Oh God!' I thought. 'Please help her, please, please do.' The consultant departed, and her curtains remained closed. An hour or two later her young man arrived, went into the cubicle and the curtains closed around him. I heard them both crying together and I could not bear it, so I went for a walk, praying and praying that things might not be too bad. How could a breast-lift seem important when a tragedy like this was taking place?

The curtains remained closed all day and through the evening, and a bed was found for the distraught boyfriend, who could not bear to leave his beloved.

Eventually, the following afternoon, the young woman opened her curtains and beckoned me over to her. We sat holding hands. Apparently she had told her consultant that she was planning her wedding in October, and he had simply said that she shouldn't make too many plans as it was unlikely to take place. She said this calmly, as if it were simply a *fait accompli*, and I marvelled at her courage.

After I left the hospital I visited her every day, taking her books by Bernie Siegel and other uplifting and comforting writers on the grim subject of illness and death. She left and returned to the country, promising to keep in touch. This proved difficult as my phone was still cut off, but I managed to reach her a few times from a call box – an unsatisfactory state of affairs. She was hopeful that things would improve and planned to see a healer. That is all I know.

My operation went very well and I now had a reasonable pair of breasts. There had been little pain involved, and I was treated with the same care and attention as those having a mastectomy.

On my last night there, something quite shattering occurred. It was announced on the Six O'Clock News that Ms Bottomley had placed the Royal Marsden on her hit list. Nobody who was not there at the time could fully appreciate the consternation, the disbelief turning to anger, that this news aroused. Patients and staff both were outraged. It was disconcerting to see the staff, normally so reassuring and positive, suddenly looking to the future of their hospital, one they were proud to work in.

I just thought that Virginia had gone mad. I had always been aware politics affected me in a practical way – my tax money might contribute to a nuclear submarine, for example. But this was something new. I almost felt as if it was a personal slap in the face – a violation of my human rights, and I decided that I would fight, using any means necessary to save the hospital.

For the next few months I worked with the 'Save the Marsden' team, getting signatures on petitions and contacting influential friends who I thought might help. One event we organized was a demonstration, a march starting in Hyde Park and finishing in Trafalgar Square, where there would be speeches. To my consternation I was asked to be one of the speakers. It was all very well working behind the scenes, but to speak in public was a terrifying prospect.

Many years previously I had been asked to take part in a twenty-four-hour vigil against nuclear weapons in Trafalgar Square. I had chosen three in the morning for my twenty-minute slot, correctly assuming that there would be no one there to see me make a fool of myself! This was going to be quite different. I begged Jemma to make the speech for me; after all, she had experience of speaking in public, but she refused. *I* was the one who had cancer, she said, and *I* should be the one to speak.

Nervously I sat down to write a speech. After I had rewritten it several times I felt quite comfortable about it. I rang Corin and read it to him, and he said it was very good so that gave me confidence. My brother Patrick, who was used to speaking in public, also thought it was excellent. Corin explained to me that when you speak into a microphone it is important to keep a measured tone; histrionics were out. So, armed with this information, I set off on the march, which was led by Fiona Fullerton, who had campaigned for years to raise money for the hospital, and Jemma. On our arrival in

Trafalgar Square I looked up at Old Nelson on his column and reckoned that I would rather be with him on his quarterdeck in the thick of battle than addressing the crowds!

Eventually it was my turn to speak. I said, 'Good morning,' into the microphone, and as my voice echoed back to me it made me jump with fright. As I was wearing a green coat I imagined I must look like a frog. However, I soon got the hang of it and the speech was very well received. I thought back to the many times I had seen Vanessa and Corin address a crowd like this. I had never dreamed that one day I would be up there.

We won! – the Marsden was saved, and I was proud to have been a part of it all.

5

My Life pre Cancer

'There is a tide in the affairs of men,
Which, taken at the flood, leads on to fortune;
Omitted, all the voyage of their life
Is bound in shallows and in miseries.'

So says Brutus in Shakespeare's *Julius Caesar*.

When I first heard those lines I felt I could have written them myself. I have found myself in shallows aplenty. Not miseries so much, but certainly shallows. I never recognized the tide, let alone the flood, even when it was right under my nose. Even if I had perceived it, I would have lacked the confidence to have ridden on the crest.

When studying the Parable of the Talents at my convent, I always felt sorry for the servant who, instead of going forth to multiply his talent, had hidden it in order to *play safe*. He was scared of losing the thing and took what he felt was a sensible course of action, only to have the wrath of his master come down on his head. I identified with him far more closely than with those who had confidently gone forth multiplying all over the place.

I was brought up to regard the word 'ambition' (a strong desire for success, achitvement or distinction) with suspicion and mistrust unless, of course, it was on the sports field. Both my parents had excelled at sports and my father had played rugger for England; but ambition in other spheres was considered to be slightly vulgar in our household.

This meant that dreams of gleaming spires, or even of the glittering lights of Broadway, were definitely out. No, my teenage yearnings simply revolved around some prat I had met, and when the said prat would ring next. Hours were spent agonizing to girlfriends on the phone about said prat. And that was that.

I find admitting this quite shocking. I mean, what would Julie Burchill make of it? But that is how it was, and it was with this appallingly limited vision that I arrived in London in the late fifties to take my place in 'Society'.

Like me, most of my contemporaries had no direction, no aims, no imagination. We were simply required to hang around meeting the 'right kind' of people until we settled down with the 'right kind' of chap. It is impossible to conceive nowadays that we had all been programmed for *nothing*. But that is how it was then. We floated around, typing, modelling or waitressing in coffee bars to keep a roof over our heads, our futures mapped out for us in precisely the same way as our parents' had been. Don't make waves, don't buck the system. The boring script for one's life was written – or so it seemed.

But something *was* happening, things *were* changing: the first great explosion of youth culture was on its way to save us. For the first time youth became a force to be reckoned with, not just an interim stage between childhood and adulthood. It was a teenage generation's declaration of independence. Young people of all backgrounds came together to embrace the subversive and seductive philosophies that were arriving from across the Atlantic – most explosively in music form, but also in films and literature.

We were Blitz babies, war-wounded children whose peaceful childhood had been wrenched from them. Terrifying memories of explosions, sirens, screams, searchlights haunted us and, worse, the forced evacuation from family life. We had been lonely children; no parental bonding for us. Now we were bonding together to change the fabric of society.

As we grew up, we were an alienated generation. We were ripe for change. Nowadays people seem to think that it was the sixties which was the time of the youth revolution. Not so. We were the ones who broke new ground, who paved the way culturally and politically for the changes to come, the 'Absolute Beginners' of Colin MacInnes's best-selling novel of the time.

We didn't drink because adults did that. Coffee bars were classless places where you met young people from all sides of the tracks. The stifling class system was beginning to crumble and you mixed with people because you liked them, not because they were 'suitable'. Indeed, the more unsuitable they were, the more you were fascinated by them. You could be anyone you wanted to, discarding your past like a dead skin. You would meet some guy in a coffee bar, and he would say, 'I was born on a freight train. I'm just a kid from nowhere,' as he placed his Woody Guthrie album very carefully on the table!

It was quite wonderful to live in London in the late fifties. The atmosphere was buzzing with expectation and excitement. Young people had enough money to begin to influence fashion and music. Jobs were plentiful, housing cheap, and no one gave a damn about the future because the present was fine.

I was sharing a house in Chelsea (Chelsea and Soho were *the* places to live) with top model Ros Watkins, the Shrimpton of her day, and drama student Gloria Kindersley, who was in the same class at Webber Douglas as Terence Stamp and Samantha Eggar. It quickly became a centre for anyone who, like us, was joining the revolution.

As with all emerging groups, it was important to be *seen* to be part of it, and one crucial identity badge was the right kind of jeans. None of your designer rubbish for us – not that it existed then anyway. Oh, no, your jeans had to be works of art: you had to get them to look as if you had just strolled away from a chain gang in the American Deep South.

First, you had to track down some obscure person who imported American Levi's, and you jealously guarded his identity. You would buy them a size too big because they shrank, then you would put them on and sit in the bath for hours until they clung to you like a second skin, scrubbing them all the while with a pumice stone and a nailbrush. They ended up looking patchy, as if you had had them for years. But then, how to get them off? You had to roll around the floor, pulling and tugging until you nearly had a heart attack with the exertion of it all. But the end result was well worth it and you could lope down the King's Road as cool as could be, them there jeans proclaiming you were part of the scene, hoping to catch the eye of one of the many Leaders of the Pack who were loping up and down similarly attired.

Apart from the jeans, there were other *de rigueur* props: a copy of *The Catcher in the Rye*, well worn, protruded from your pocket; an album or two under your arm showed that you were no novice – Lambert, Hendricks and Ross, and Mose Allison were considered 'cool'. Cool was the name of the game.

Other required reading were books by Kerouac, Jean-Paul Sartre and Steinbeck. Films to discuss earnestly over a cappuccino were *On the Waterfront*, *Rebel Without a Cause*, and *East of Eden*. In the theatre there was *Fings Ain't What They Used t'Be* and, of course, *Look Back in Anger*. The anti-hero had become a sex symbol. Goodbye Doris and Rock for ever.

And then came rock 'n' roll. Hail, hail, rock 'n' roll! It exploded upon our sleeping senses like an atomic bomb. The raw energy of it, the raunchy, swaggering sexuality of it, the animal magnetism of it, the subversive lyrics, the sight of Elvis gyrating and jerking as if he were plugged into an electric socket, the snarling, brooding sensuality of his son-of-the-soil face, handsome beyond belief; it all promised sexual abandonment beyond our wildest dreams. 'If you're looking for trouble,' he howled, 'then you've come to the right place!'

Well, we were looking for trouble! Into the bin went twin sets and Jaeger suits. The pearls were pawned and the money spent on black stockings, as much mascara as your eyelashes could handle, and nights spent in some Soho dive, jiving until dawn.

A direction had been found for some of us aimless young women. It was to become rebels, and the time was right. Politically uneducated, we started our journey to the Left by demonstrating against the bomb. We marched from Aldermaston to Trafalgar Square to make our protest against this threat to our future, having experienced war at first hand in our childhood. Here it was that I first saw my future sister-in-law, Vanessa, giving an impassioned speech, which inspired me greatly.

It has been said that the New Left in America sprang from Elvis's gyrating pelvis and, being politically naive, I also took my lead from him. The sheer anarchy of his music and his movements inspired a generation to want to buck the complacent, arrogant system in power, and replace it with an exciting and positive system, based on youthful values. According to Thoreau, 'Youth gathers together the material to build a bridge to the moon. Maturity uses it to build a woodshed.'

Not everyone was changing, though. One evening I went out to dinner with an old friend, an army officer. (The Leaders of the Pack were not great at buying one dinner!) During our meal he came out with: 'You know that I've been stationed in Germany? Well, a jolly funny thing happened while I was there. One day I picked up a young American soldier whose jeep had broken down and gave him a lift for a hundred miles or so. When I dropped him off I said to him that, jolly strange as it might seem, I thought I knew his face. "Thank you for the ride, sir," said the young GI. "My name is Elvis Presley." What do you think of that?'

Well, I didn't think too much of it at all. It certainly was not 'jolly funny'. Notwithstanding my hunger, I was out of the restaurant like a jack rabbit. I simply couldn't believe that cool ole me could find myself in such 'square' company.

Life was so adventurous and exciting that I always felt sorry for girlfriends who left the scene to settle down and get married. But soon I was to make a commitment which would dramatically change the rest of my life.

I had heard a great deal about Corin Redgrave before we met. His best friend at Westminster, Jonathan Benson, had regaled me with stories about his brilliant intellect and wicked sense of humour, so when Corin came down from Cambridge to star in a play at the Royal Court Theatre, Jonathan arranged for us to go and see it. I had known Jonathan for many years, having met him in Malta where he was doing his National Service. We were close friends.

That evening in 1962 we set off to see Tony Richardson's production of *A Midsummer Night's Dream* starring Corin, his sister Lynn, Nicol Williamson, Rita Tushingham, Samantha Eggar and David Warner – all the up and coming stars of the future.

It is strange, looking back, to realize that in 1962 Sir Michael was the only really famous member of the family, with Vanessa just emerging as a star at Stratford. Nowadays the family is referred to as a theatrical dynasty: new, talented members are continually being hailed as they take their place on the boards.

After the performance, Corin, Jonathan and I set out for dinner at a trendy Chelsea restaurant. One thing Jonathan had omitted to tell me about Corin was how good looking he was, rather like Jean-Paul Belmondo. But he had only to set one foot inside the restaurant for me to see that this was not the sort of place he was used to. I was watching carefully, and as we walked to our table through the throng, many of whom greeted Jonathan and me, the expression on his face was wary, verging on contemptuous. As I glanced around I could see how my 'dashing rebels' looked like a bunch of fools to him, and I began to feel like one too.

I remained quiet as he and Jonathan discussed writers, painters and philosophers I had never heard of. The more arrogant and disdainful Corin appeared, the more intrigued I became. When I did speak, everything I said came out sounding idiotic. Corin was deliberately ignoring me, and I was not used to being ignored.

I bided my time until Jonathan went off to the loo, and then I looked at him long and hard. 'Does making other people uncomfortable give you some strange satisfaction?' I asked. He just stared back at me and we made eye contact for the first time; for a long time.

As the evening progressed I had an intuitive feeling that this man was going to mean something apocalyptic in my life. There was a current between us that had not been acknowledged by him until I had spoken to him alone.

Jonathan was surprised when Corin invited us back to the Redgraves' for a drink; his friend had always seemed the unsociable type. But I was not surprised: it was inevitable.

At the flat in Knightsbridge, Corin and Jonathan continued to exclude me from their conversation, but one thing had changed. At dinner Corin had barely glanced at me; now I could feel his eyes continually slanting away from Jonathan and resting on me. Eventually he wandered over to the grand piano and started to play the tough card sharp's song that Brando sings to Jean Simmons in the film *Guys and Dolls*.

When he reached the lines: 'My time of day is the night time, a couple of deals before dawn ... and you're the only doll I've ever wanted to share it with me, alone,' he never took his eyes from my face. There and then I fell in love with him.

Within six months of our first meeting we were married. Having taken me out to dinner one evening, he invited me once more to the flat for a drink. He opened a bottle of champagne and drew me out on to the balcony. It was a romantic starry night, and as we stood sipping our champagne the air was filled with expectancy. He turned to speak to me when there was an almighty roar from Sir Michael, furious at being woken up, and at Corin for taking a bottle of his champagne. An almighty roar from a knight of the theatre is enough to frighten you half to death so, having dropped my glass over the balcony and heard an infuriated shout from the street below, I fled, promising Corin that I would meet him for lunch at Prunier's in St James's the following day. My first meeting with Rachel had been even more spectacularly embarrassing: early on in our relationship Corin invited me out to dinner and then on to a nightclub. I borrowed a stunning emerald satin suit from my flatmate Gloria, donned my stilettos, black stockings, false eyelashes, and set off for a night on the town. We had a magical evening – a delicious dinner followed by a bit of twisting – and in the early hours we set off for home. Corin was driving a red fifties Ford Thunderbird convertible, the kind that brings Chuck Berry to mind, and as we drove through the warm spring night I realized how much in love with him I was. I did not want this to be a passing fancy; no, I knew I wanted to marry him. In those days, that was how things were done, and anyway, I was far too insecure even to have entertained the idea of living with him.

As we drove through the silent London streets Corin persuaded me, much against my better judgement, not to go home, but to accompany him to his parents' cottage in Hampshire for the weekend. It was an offer I couldn't refuse, although I made every excuse in the book: I didn't have any suitable clothes, I didn't want to meet his family in these circumstances, and so on; but he assured me that his family were away, and that we could be alone for once. I couldn't resist him.

As we sped through the leafy Hampshire lanes, listening to Mozart (not really in keeping with a red fifties Ford Thunderbird convertible, but I was not complaining), I lay back and looked up at the clear starry sky and experienced a feeling of elation mixed with fear that I might prove an inadequate companion over a couple of days, and that this blissful romance might end.

The cottage was as charming and idyllic as Corin had claimed. I felt nervous: it was the first time I had been completely on his territory, and I loved it so much that I wanted to be part of his family all the more. As the dawn chill settled over the meadows, Corin lit the log fire and we sipped wine and talked till daybreak.

Set in the cottage gardens was a studio where Michael would stay for the occasional weekend; he usually preferred the cosmopolitan life. It was situated by the Redgraves' private lake, and it was there, in that magical place, that I spent my first night with Corin.

I awoke the next morning to find the sun streaming through the studio windows. Corin had disappeared, but had placed a red rose by my pillow, and I was touched by this romantic gesture: I knew it was to reassure me about his feelings for me. It meant that I was not a one-night stand.

Corin appeared in the doorway carrying a breakfast tray, beaming. 'Mum and Lynn have arrived,' he said. 'I am so longing for you to meet them.'

I had, of course, been hoping to meet them as well, but not in these circumstances. I looked in the mirror beside the bed and saw that I had mascara streaked down my face and that one false eyelash was still gamely clinging on. I was horrified. The night before I had dressed up like all kinds of a slut — perfect for a smoky nightclub; but here, on a fine Sunday morning in the country, I looked and felt like a tramp. I could imagine my mother, if my brothers had turned up with girls looking like me. They would have stood no chance. 'I won't meet them looking like this,' I protested. 'No way! I simply won't.'

'Well, what are you going to do, then?' asked an angry Corin.

'I'll slip away through the woods and hitch a lift back to London. When I meet your family I want it to be right, not like this.'

The magic of the night had evaporated, and this was our first row. Corin called me a silly bourgeois fool, and explained that his family were not small-minded, judgemental, petty, provincial people as my family clearly must be. Well, my crying did not help the mascara situation, but after a while, through a mixture of cajoling and bullying, he persuaded me to emerge from the studio, my fine emerald satin suit positively strobing in the bright morning sunshine.

I walked across the lawn, my stilettos getting stuck in the turf at every step. To add to it all, I noticed a large ladder in my black stocking. A weekend guest from hell.

But Corin had been quite right: my extraordinary appearance did not throw Rachel or Lynn at all. Lynn offered to take me up to her room to borrow some clothes and remove my smeared make-up.

I rejoined Corin and Rachel in the garden, where we sat sipping white wine under the apple trees. Rachel was very beautiful and had the slender, lithe body of a young girl. Her energy and charm had me spellbound, and I discovered that my naval background meant that we had many friends in common: her father had been headmaster at Dartmouth, where all the young midshipmen had been in love with her. The warm rapport we established on that first meeting has never diminished. Through all my ups and downs she has remained a source of strength and love; she is simply the best mum-in-law one could have.

Lynn and I also quickly developed a firm friendship. She was still at drama school, a very amusing person who treated me like an older sister to whom she could confide all the problems she was having with boys. Well, she had found an expert on that topic!

When Corin and I departed on the Sunday evening, both Rachel and Lynn hugged me and invited me to stay the next weekend. The ice had been well and truly broken.

At Prunier's, over lobster and more champagne, Corin asked me if I would marry him. With unutterable happiness and tears in my eyes, I said yes.

We were both very young, and I know that Michael and Rachel had their reservations, especially as Corin had started out on a glittering career, but we were so in love that they soon happily accepted our marriage.

My parents flew over from Malta to meet their prospective son-in-law, and they and Michael and Rachel got on very well. Rachel knew many of my father's naval friends. She confided to me that she thought that Dad was just about the handsomest man she had ever met.

The wedding was held in the actor's church, St Paul's Covent Garden, the service marred only by the vicar calling me Desirée (which I thought was great, an improvement on Deirdre if ever I heard one!), with Corin firmly correcting him each time.

Ours was a true attraction of opposites. Corin was seriously ambitious and excelled not only in the academic field but also in sports, music, and in the theatre. He was a bad loser, even when playing a friendly game of tennis, and I came in for a lot of abuse when I fluffed an easy shot or served double faults throughout a game. I was learning that I really had to make an effort to match his expectations of me - and he had many. I was constantly aware of my lack of formal education, but what I had failed to realize, as I swatted over literary and theatrical reviews in an effort to hold my own in conversation with him, was that he was doing the same thing – reading books on jazz and buying Ray Charles albums. Looking back, it all seems rather touching.

Corin believed that my flippancy belied a wealth of untapped talent and that I had a good brain, so I became his Eliza Dolittle as he encouraged me to believe in myself. All this was salutary for me as I was entering a new and testing milieu.

Vanessa was married to director Tony Richardson, and they were the golden couple of the *avant garde*. Tony at that time was directing *Tom Jones*, and Vee was still at Stratford. Their dinner parties were always full of people I was in awe of – John Osborne, Alan Bates, George Devine, among others, and I listened hard, trying to learn from them and become part of this new world.

Corin was now starring in Arnold Wesker's *Chips with Everything* and talented old me was working in the evening as a waitress to supplement our income and keep the same hours as he did.

In the beginning I felt insecure. I seemed to have little to contribute to all these iconoclasts, but Corin reassured me that this was not so, and that he felt very proud of me. Another great supporter was Tony Richardson. He understood my feelings and went out of his way to give me confidence. We remained very close long after his divorce from Vanessa and mine from Corin.

We entertained a lot, and one evening John Hurt and his then wife, Annette Robertson, came for dinner. During the meal John asked Corin what his aim in life was. 'Being for ever happy with Deirdre,' Corin replied.

John looked surprised and told us: 'The most important aim in my life is to become a successful actor.' This of course led to a furious row between the Hurts! Still, it is John's dream that came true.

Lynn and I were fast becoming close friends, so one summer when she had just finished *Georgy Girl*, the film that launched her career, she came out to stay with me and my family in Malta for a much-needed holiday. Late one afternoon, as we were sunning ourselves on my father's yacht, she said a strange thing: 'I have never met a father who appears to ignore his daughter so much, apart from my own.' She was the only person who had ever observed my father's inability to communicate with me. I suppose it takes one to know one, and we talked and talked about our problem. I adored my father, but when I grew up and became a young woman he found it difficult to cope. This is a common problem in English fathers of that generation: they fear their daughters' obvious sexuality, they are jealous of their boyfriends, and so they withdraw their affection.

This was further compounded in my father's case because I was such a rebel. Many of his friends' daughters were nice young girls, all proper and how they should be, and I am sure he wished I was more like them.

A friend of Dad's once lent him *Lolita* to read. He started it but was so alarmed by the content that he burnt it in the fireplace. Then, being well mannered, he had to buy another copy to return.

My mother was a much more adventurous reader. When she came to stay with us she slept in Corin's study/library and would appear at breakfast saying that she had not slept a wink because she had read all night. She would talk to me enthusiastically about books that were quite new to her – George Orwell, for instance. Corin once made an interesting observation about her: 'I have never met anyone who reads so avidly,' he said, 'but is so unchanged by what they read.' I, on the other hand, was deeply affected by anything I read, my perceptions changing author by author.

Both my parents were Irish. My mother came from an Anglo-Irish family in County Kildare; my father's ancestors, the Hamiltons, from Killyleagh Castle in County Down.

When my father retired, he and Mum came to settle in England and he made a point of seeing something of me on my own. To my delight, for the first time he wanted to get to know me and we would have lunch once a week. It was a great relief. All the emotions that we had both stifled over the years were now, finally, set free. He was really interested in my political beliefs, and this time there were no witty put-downs at my expense. I also asked him about his childhood, the war and his life in general, and the exchange was very rewarding. The barriers went down, and respect, pride and love flowed between us.

When friends cling on to their prejudices against their ageing parents I always advise them to try and find a way through them, however disinclined they might be. When my father died, six months to the day after my mother, I could let him go in peace. There was no guilt or resentment; only joyful memories.

Lynn was not so fortunate in resolving her conflicts with her father. She lived in America during Michael's later years, and therefore had no opportunity to bridge the gap, as I had with my father. However, she did find a way of coming to terms with her feelings: she wrote and starred in her own one-woman show, *Shakespeare for My Father*, to great critical acclaim. A huge and therapeutic success for her, and a marvellous tribute to Michael.

Corin was keen to start a family and in 1965 our daughter Jemma was born. During the pregnancy I spent a lot of time with Vanessa, who was expecting Joely, and Jemma and she arrived within three days of each other. Vee was a fund of information on how to deal with swollen ankles, indigestion, sleepless nights and the sudden cold moments of apprehension that assailed me in the middle of the night. At last I was getting to really know the person who, apart from me, was closest in the world to Corin.

Luke was born in 1967. We had moved to a large mansion flat in Coleherne Court (of Lady Di fame) and I settled happily into my new role as mother. I blossomed. At last I had an identity and I loved it.

Many of my friends who had not married had become staunch feminists. They were outraged at my attitude, and I found their fury daunting. Of course I read the books and went along with some of their philosophy, but I could not see that adoring motherhood was a crime. Furthermore, I really liked men – but I kept that to myself for fear of apoplexy on the part of the man-haters I knew.

One evening, though, I had a highly amusing evening with the sisters. I had been invited by a feminist friend to attend a party at the ICA Gallery to celebrate a feminist theatre festival. This friend was very beautiful. I had seen her in a feminist play, in which she always played the part of the 'dreadful woman' who was an example of what *not* to be. The dreadful woman had perfect make-up and hair and was dressed in designer clothes. The rest of the cast looked like ugly lumps, which was, of course, the right way to look. My friend *hated* playing that part, she said ... oh yeah?

As I did not possess any dungarees, I arrived in a pair of jeans to find a room filled with frightening-looking women, except for my friend, who was as glamorous as always! This was to be an all-woman bash apart from a male theatre group called the Wee Wees! The Wee Wees? I ask you.

Now this was the early seventies when punk had not yet been heard of. Malcolm McLaren was spreading his subversive word in underground clubs; his Sex Pistols had not yet emerged into the daylight. Anyway, the lights dimmed and on to the stage roared a group of youths covered in safety pins and tattoos of the most sexist nature, screaming obscenities. They started playing their guitars and singing lyrics that went something like this: 'You c—s should all be getting f—g laid.'

Well, pandemonium broke out among the sisters. Cries of '*Shame, shame!*' rang out from all sides; women were running about shouting and yelling. The band stopped playing in complete bewilderment. For all their macho exterior, they looked quite terrified – and who could blame them? It was a terrifying sight!

By this time I had dissolved in laughter. What a confrontation! It was reminiscent of King Kong versus Godzilla! The more I laughed the more the sisters screamed abuse at me as well as at the band. Lordy, lordy, lordy, Miss Claudy, whatever happened to a sense of humour! I am well aware that feminist politics are serious but this was so ludicrous!

Seeing that I was not shouting with fury, the young bass player came over to me in total bemusement, and asked me to explain what was going on. How do you explain feminist rage to a sixteen-year-old punk who has never even heard of the word?

The cries of '*Shame, shame!*' continued and then a chant

went up, 'Who booked the band? Who booked the band?!' and as I crept away from the scene I saw a petrified woman getting a severe roasting from the sisters.

Corin was a loving husband and father and generous to a fault. One birthday, he took me down to the street, where I found a stylish convertible waiting for me. 'It's yours, Dee,' he said. 'Do you like it?' He was always surprising me with gifts and outings to the theatre and restaurants. Most weekends we went to stay at his mother's cottage. The children loved being there, and it was wonderful to get them away from an urban environment. They were taught country lore by her gardener, who was an old gypsy, so they grew up with a love of the country as well as becoming streetwise. I spent some of the happiest times of my life there, but things were about to change.

For many years Corin and I had shared the same political beliefs: we had demonstrated against the bomb and the war in Vietnam and we were present at the battle of Grosvenor Square. We had helped Black Power groups in their struggle for justice, and worked against the system of apartheid. But now, at the end of the sixties, like many left-wing intellectuals of his generation, Corin found that his political perspective had altered. He referred to what we had taken part in as 'Cause Politics'. It was time, he said, to work against injustice from within a structured framework, and he found exactly what he was looking for in the Socialist Labour League (later to become the Workers Revolutionary Party).

As the party absorbed him more and more he began to spend less and less time at home with his family. I was terrified. One weekend I begged him to come with me and the children to the cottage for a break. He looked at me sadly but resolutely. 'Dee,' he said, 'you *must* understand, our halcyon days are over.' A chilling prophecy.

I tried my best to go along with him by attending party meetings and reading recommended books. At one meeting, a young woman put her hand up. 'What will be the role of spirituality in England once the revolution has succeeded?' she asked nervously. It was a question I had wanted to ask.

'We are not here to waste our time on middle-class rubbish!' shouted Gerry Healy, the party's leader.

I saw that the woman had tears in her eyes, and I felt like crying too. Another nail in the coffin.

The more committed Corin became, the lonelier I felt. At least Tory and Labour ministers' wives understood their husbands' politics, but I was in uncharted territories. Corin was adamant: 'Dee, you are either with us or against us in our struggle.' I didn't know what to say. I was so scared.

However, there was one person who was not at all scared: my mother. She was very fond of Corin, and they had always got on well, but now her general attitude infuriated him. As the saying goes, 'Humour is the last bastion of the bourgeoisie!' She would come out with appallingly annoying things like, 'Tell me, Corin, when you are in power will I be like the Queen Mother and have the Royal Box at Ascot?' . . . 'Perhaps I could run Hampshire!' Worst of all: 'You've been stirring up the workmen again, Corin. My plumber was frightfully rude to me this morning.' All guaranteed to exasperate a true Marxist.

She was also convinced that the actor/writer party member Tom Kempinski (author of *Duet for One*) was in fact called Tom Kemp, and that he had added the 'inski' as an affectation.

Mum did make me laugh, although this truly was no laughing matter. In the beginning I was able to talk to Vanessa about my worries. She was concerned too, but eventually she joined the League. She couldn't understand that I simply found it impossible to accept all the dictates of the party, and she was hurt on Corin's behalf. Another person close to me had closed a door, and I missed her friendship.

Lynn was living in America, so I turned to my mother-in-law, Rachel. I had always loved her dearly, and she was a great shoulder to cry on. She understood my increasing isolation from the family, and went out of her way to invite me down to the cottage whenever possible. She loved and admired Corin, and respected the choices he was making, but she could also see that I was being hurt by them. She took no sides, but supported us both.

I was now confronted with Corin's ultimatum. To join or not to join. Although my husband was an eloquent teacher, and I agreed with the Communist Manifesto, I simply could not follow him down his chosen path – at least, not all the way, and he meant all or nothing.

I panicked, knowing that this would all lead inevitably to a parting of the ways. Loving him as I did, it was the last thing I wanted and, to be fair, the last thing *he* wanted, but the gulf between us grew and grew.

The final parting of the ways came about at Christmas 1974. On Christmas Day we were both numb with pain, but Corin stayed until Boxing Day and we both tried to be normal for the children's sake. I will never forget watching him as, ashen faced, he packed his suitcase. We couldn't speak. As he walked away down the corridor, shoulders hunched, it took all my strength not to run after him, hold him and say that everything was all right and that he should come home. But I knew nothing would change and so did he. It is very hard to break up when you still love each other so much, but Corin, who had taught me so much, and with whom I had shared so many wonderful years and two children, had moved on down a new path – a path it was impossible for me to take.

We did not get a divorce for many years. I suspect that neither of us wanted that finality, and I might otherwise have taken the disastrous step of getting married to some unsuitable man. Eventually, in 1985, it was Corin who wanted to marry his new love, the actress Kika Markham, who shared his political beliefs and had borne him two sons.

I went alone to the divorce courts. It was a trip to hell: couples glaring and shouting at each other in fear and loathing. They must have loved each other once. What a sad sight.

Ours was a very amicable divorce. In the courtroom I spoke so warmly of Corin that the Judge observed he was surprised we were separating. Still, I cried all the way home in the car. The finality of it. The death of young dreams.

Before our separation, when both the children were at school full time, I had decided to get a job. A girlfriend and I rented a stall in Antiquarius in the King's Road, where we sold antique clothing: twenties and thirties evening clothes in lace, satin or embroidered with sequins, Victorian nighties, forties crêpe dresses with accessories such as hats, shoes and jewellery – all very popular in the seventies. As 'glam rock' was fashionable in those days pop stars would buy from us: Freddie Mercury and Robert Plant were regular customers.

It was marvellous to be in this colourful place every day, and to get away from the problems of our marriage. It felt good to be earning money again, and not have to ask Corin for every penny. Our stall was like a grown-up's dressing-up box, every little girl's dream. I was meeting new people and beginning to feel more like my own self. If I had to, I could confront the future alone.

After we split up it was up to me to forge a new life for myself and the children. One major problem was that Corin had stopped working to devote all his energies to his politics, and I was certainly not earning enough money on my stall to support the three of us.

With the knowledge of period clothing I had acquired at Antiquarius, I started working as a stylist on films and commercials. The work was highly demanding and stressful, but it was creative and highly paid and happily kept the wolf from our door.

The only problem with the job was that it was freelance, and there were times when I was out of work for quite a while. This meant I had to sign on. What a nightmare that proved to be! When you have a surname like Redgrave, people simply assume that you are reasonably well heeled. Not so. I have frequently found myself in the poverty trap, then emerged from it only to return once again to the mire. Because of my surname, I always felt self-conscious in the dole office. One day, I was in a queue with many others when my name was called by a voice like a foghorn: 'Would Mrs *Redgrave* please come over to booth two?' Everyone turned to look at me, so I slipped over in a pool of Special Brew. Now I not only felt like a vagrant, I smelt like a vagrant! It was all very upsetting.

Occasionally I would find myself at a dinner party where the other guests mocked 'scroungers', as they called those on Income Support; of course they had no idea that I was one of them. I hated their smug, self-satisfied attitude to life. They had never taken risks, and I found their contempt for people less well off than themselves sickening. Their aspirations were solely materialistic, and I had nothing in common with them. I stopped pretending to be upwardly mobile, and dumped that circle for ever.

Now that I was single, I began going out on dates. Having married very young – having, in fact, been married right through the sixties – it was exciting to go dancing again. At clubs and parties I rediscovered many of the old friends I had lost touch with during Corin's strict regime of our last years together. I felt younger than I had in years. I was working very hard and playing hard, too. Old friends started drifting back to the flat. Once again our home rang with music and laughter.

Suddenly I was getting attention and flattery and I began to blossom. I was no longer what some of the League members made me feel, merely a silly woman who could not understand why Marxism had to rule the planet. My self-confidence, which had been severely eroded, began to return. Life was good and, over the years, I had several liaisons, some delightfully *dangereuse*, some dull, but I had never seriously considered getting married again until I met Jeffrey Bernard. The year was 1985. I was an occasional reader of the *Spectator* and knew who he was, and it was brought to my attention that he had written a very nasty column about stupid women who stand up in Trafalgar Square to denounce the bomb, in which he included my name. I was furious, and resolved that if I ever met him, I would let him know what I thought of him. The cause of nuclear disarmament was very important to me.

One evening he was interviewed on television, and much to my surprise he came across as charming and witty. Without doubt he was the best-looking man I had ever seen. I determined to meet him.

I was told that he drank daily in a pub called the Coach and Horses in Soho, so the next time I was working on a commercial near by I dropped in with a girlfriend in the hope of finding him.

John Hurt was there and joined us for a drink, but my eyes were on the door. Then in he came, even better looking than he had appeared on television. He ordered a drink and then kept looking at me until finally he came over and asked John to introduce him.

I refused to shake the offered hand, saying, 'Mr Bernard,

you insulted me in one of your "Low Life" columns, therefore I cannot shake your hand.'

He looked quite bemused and, as he told me later, retired to his chair to rethink his approach. Back he came, saying, 'Last night I won the Journalist of the Year Award. To make amends to you, would you join me for a champagne lunch they are giving me in Kettners?' We departed to Kettners, and I felt I was walking on air. How could it have been so easy? At the restaurant people kept coming up to congratulate him on the award, and the champagne flowed.

When all his friends had gone, Jeffrey suddenly looked at me very intently. 'I would very much like to make love to you,' he said. He is not one to beat about the bush.

I summoned up all the hauteur I could muster. 'I am not a one-night stand,' I replied, at which he took my hand, gazed at me with his beautiful blue eyes and said, 'I don't mean for one night, I mean for a thousand and one nights!'

Well, that was that. To my horror I heard myself say, 'Jeffrey, I want to drown in your eyes.' I mean, can you imagine saying such a thing? No wonder I am quite good at writing Mills and Boons!

The conversation went from bad to worse, as far as I was concerned. Having ordered our meal Jeffrey embarked on his favourite topic – sex. He was discussing the differences between sleeping with upper-class and working-class women. This was all a bit too quick for me, but I tried to appear sophisticated about it. 'Working-class women are different,' he said, then paused and continued, 'They're very slow in coming!'

With as much composure as I could muster I enquired, 'Are upper-class women quicker then?' whereupon he turned on me and said, 'I was talking about the service.'

Oh, earth, open up, please open up, earth, I prayed, feeling a complete fool. What embarrassment! As I left him to go back to work I said, 'Would you like to see me again?' After my monumental stupidity I assumed he must think me an idiot. 'One hour away from you will be too long,' he replied. I met him for dinner that same night. We had fallen in love.

It's always the same: sleepless nights, churning stomach, agonizing over everything he said, the terrifying impatience when my taxi got stuck in a traffic jam on its way to the Coach and Horses. All that old stuff felt as fresh and new as if I had never been through it before. However, this was to be a romance with a difference.

Every week Jeffrey would discuss our romance with the readers of the *Spectator* in his column (I was known as 'She Who Drown In His Eyes'), and every week I would buy my copy of the magazine with great trepidation, wondering what foolishness he would attribute to me this time round. For example:

A few minutes ago I asked She Who Would Drown In My Eyes to scramble some eggs and she complained that I treat her like a geisha girl. Then, when I went into the kitchen to console her and reassure her that Greenham Common was a wonderful shambles and that really my idea of heaven is to sit on straw bales drinking tea out of tin mugs and not hanging about at Royal Ascot swilling bubbly, she muttered something about wanting to be Carmen and not the Mary Poppins I had turned her into. My God, don't women come out with some strange stuff. One minute it's Greenham and Marxism and the next minute she announces, 'Most of my friends will be in the Royal Enclosure this week.' When the barricades go up she'll be jumping from one side to the other like a demented frog . . .

. . . When you get to be a fifty-three-year-old skeleton with grey hair you have to be grateful for small mercies. Come to think of it, she is not exactly a small mercy. She has an ample bosom and she even has legs on a par with Cyd Charisse's but she will cover them up with those awful baggy trousers . . .

These articles were a source of great hilarity to my friends. 'Demented frog, heh, heh, heh,' they would laugh; 'Mary Poppins, eh? Heh, heh, heh!' – and a great source of embarrassment to myself. It was pointless for me to ask Jeff to write something really romantic; my discomfort spurred him on to ever greater heights. Finally, after he had been particularly amusing at my expense one week, I decided to get my own back and sent the following letter to the *Spectator*.

Followers of the 'Low Life' column may be interested to learn that She Who Would Drown In Mr Jeffrey Bernard's Eyes is normally a woman of discretion. However, realizing that she has become an ongoing butt of Mr Bernard's humour, a sort of female Norman, she feels driven to point out that she, too, has a few stories to tell. Her lot is not an easy one.

For example, the other evening she arrived at the appointed hour to meet the writer for dinner – having incidentally done her very best to emulate the style of one Miss Virginia Mayo, an American cinema actress of the forties for whose talents Mr Bernard had expressed great admiration. Mr Bernard's arrival had preceded her own. Indeed, he had already eaten, and now, head on table, was sound asleep. Inviting her to order, the restaurateur assured her that this was nothing new and that her companion would wake up in an hour or two.

She Who Would Drown In Mr Bernard's Eyes felt the situation to be an appalling embarrassment but, nobly, decided to sit it out. One consideration, among many, stood out particularly. Might not the other diners assume that it was her boring conversation and that indeed she, and not the vodka, had driven him into this state of unconsciousness? Eventually Mr Bernard awoke. 'Let's go out to dinner,' he suggested enthusiastically.

She will not dwell on the matter of getting him to sign a cheque for a meal he could not remember eating. Suffice to say it could be rivalled only by that of getting a signature on the death warrant of Charles I.

Mr Bernard, trapped in a sartorial timewarp as one magazine put it, nags endlessly for stiletto heals, seamed stockings, skin-tight skirts and much cleavage. Any protest from her that the baggy look is in is met with the contempt previously reserved for anyone who thought Ascot had to do with a heating device.

Once, having massaged his pugilistic shoulders for an hour and a half, a discussion on male attitudes had developed. Refreshed, Mr Bernard leapt to his feet and as he playfully flung a crumpled shirt into her aching hands to be ironed, the words, 'Of course I'm not chauvinistic,' were heard to issue from his mouth.

Still, it is essentially the childlike quality of Mr Bernard that is so disarming. When she talked to him of the delights of parenthood, he looked at her with all the horror of one who has just seen Banquo's ghost. 'But I am a child,' he wailed. And it is this juvenile quality that restrains her from emulating one Miss Esther Williams, an American actress of the forties for whose talents Mr Bernard had expressed great admiration, and learning to swim.

Well, this letter was greeted with much acclaim by his many friends, and I received fan mail from *Spectator* readers. Jeffrey was delighted with it, and shortly after it was published he asked me to marry him. Although our relationship was very volatile, and I spent half my time on the number fourteen bus which runs from Chelsea to Soho and back in floods of tears, I couldn't say no!

The articles continued to amuse all Jeffrey's fans, and strangers would come up to me in the Coach and Horses and say things like, 'Are you really *she*?' All very Rider Haggard. Norman, the guv'ner of the Coach would croon love songs to us, and the jazz musician Barney Bates wrote a song called 'Jeffrey and Deirdre Blues'. Jeffrey himself referred to us as Jeff Mills and Deirdre Boon. It was all quite lovely, but very unreal.

Incidentally, it was on the top of the number fourteen bus that I first met Francis Bacon. Although the man is unmistakable I could not believe that Francis Bacon would be on a bus. Then I noticed the Rolex, and a suede jacket so fine that it almost looked like silk, and realized that the man had serious money. I plucked up enough courage to speak to him, and he was charming. At the end of our conversation I told him that I was engaged to marry his friend Jeffrey. He looked at me, eyes twinkling. 'That's your problem,' he said.

After many many months of this magic, as sometimes happens, we began to drift apart. 'It was just one of those things,' and, as this line summed up, 'we should have been aware that our love affair was too hot not to cool down.'

I will always be grateful to Jeffrey for the charmed time we had, the laughter we shared – a true romance at a time in life when one assumed that it was all over.

6
So What's the Meaning of Life Then?

I of'en looked up at the sky an' assed meself the question – what is the stars, what is the stars? – *Sean O'Casey*

I walked into a New Age bookshop with friend Mark. We browsed around the stacks of books covering every philosophy that you could ever think of. Totally overwhelmed by the wealth of knowledge available, Mark walked over to the elderly proprietor. 'Read all these books, have you?' he asked.

'I have, yes,' replied the old man.

'All right,' said Mark, 'so tell me, what's the meaning of life then?'

The old question, the *big* one!

Legend has it that one fine morning, St Augustine was pacing up and down a deserted beach, pondering that very problem. He meditated upon the subject, but realized that every time he thought he had hit on something, it was mere speculation.

Suddenly a small boy appeared in front of him carrying a pan of water from the ocean which he poured into a hole he had dug in the sand. 'Tell me, child,' said St Augustine, 'what is it that you are trying to do?'

'To make a pond,' replied the child.

St Augustine looked at the child thoughtfully. 'You cannot do that,' he said. 'However many pans of water you pour into the hole, it will all soak through the sand. It is impossible.'

'It is equally impossible for you to understand the meaning of the universe,' said the child.

It's quite a relief really, that legend. I mean, if St Augustine couldn't hack it, how on earth was I supposed to? Still, the *big* one never goes away, especially when one is very ill. Then, it is seriously centre stage.

It has been statistically proven that people who have a firm faith or a firm philosophy of life suffer from less tension and stress than the waverers, so it is well worth making the quest for an answer.

This chapter tells of experiences that have helped me through my doubts and scepticism (which most ex-convent girls suffer), towards a new perception – all the little things that have nudged me to a greater spiritual awareness. I feel like Sherlock Holmes, finding little clues here and there, watching out for further developments.

Although I had always been interested in the paranormal, and in studying different religious faiths, I refused point blank to become a vegan or go on a macrobiotic diet, as many of my contemporaries did; I loathed the brown rice that was invariably served up when dining with friends in the sixties. Holistic medicines I quite erroneously considered faddish. In fact my only concession to the new theories gaining ground at that time was to give up white bread for brown. How I missed those large white slabs of bread covered in unhealthy butter and treacle!

It always puzzled me, however, when friends who were perfectly happy with their drug intake became apoplectic if I put white sugar in their coffee instead of brown. Who were they trying to kid! 'The killer whites' they would say smugly, as if they didn't have plenty of 'killer whites' going up their nose or down their throat.

I am only going to talk here about my own experiences,

since bookshops are brimming over with fine books that cover every aspect of alternative healing and the paranormal. My life has been immeasurably enriched by many things that are beyond our ken.

It cannot be said that sighting a UFO has anything to do with spiritual advancement; however, it does fall into the 'Tales of the Unexpected' category, so here goes. I will add my name to the long list of people (President Carter and John Lennon, amongst others) who claim to have seen one.

In the mid seventies I was enjoying a holiday on the Norfolk Broads with Jemma (ten), Luke (eight) and my then boyfriend, Johnny. We had hired a boat, and apart from hitting the odd sand bank and careering into jetties when attempting to moor, we were having a great time. One evening we had finished dinner and Johnny and the kids were watching TV while I was gazing dreamily out of the window. It was a clear night, not a cloud to be seen. Suddenly I noticed what looked like a small white object zigzagging across the heavens. At my summons, the others came and joined me at the window. We decided that it was probably a reflection from the water. However, we trooped up on deck, Johnny taking his binoculars with him.

This zigzagging white ball of light was no reflection. As we watched, it suddenly stopped still. Now this was way above the normal flight zone; it could not possibly have been a plane or a helicopter. As we stood watching, a bright light, conical in shape, beamed downwards from the craft. I thought I saw small dark shapes emerge from this light but that could be my fertile imagination. Anyway, the beam disappeared, and then, strangest of all, it appeared that the white ball of light had become a beacon. A revolving light poured forth from it, changing colour, from white to green, yellow and orange, at each rotation.

We all took turns with the binoculars and saw that this was no imagining on our part. Whatever it was looked real enough, yet we were not frightened in the least. On the contrary, it felt comforting to know that we were not the only people in our great universe.

After about ten minutes the revolving light disappeared. The white ball remained motionless in the sky, then shot straight upwards at great speed until it disappeared from sight.

We returned to the cabin to talk over what we had seen. All four of us had identical stories so we could be sure that it was not just one person's hallucination. It was all very exciting.

Back home, I checked with UFO buffs I knew to see what they thought about our sighting. They explained to me that it was a typical manifestation of the phenomenon, even down to the changing colour of the light.

All this has taught me never to dismiss out of hand apparently inexplicable events. However, I have never yet seen a corn circle!

Nowadays it is perfectly acceptable to own up to having had an out-of-body experience. Indeed books are written on the subject, sometimes by surgeons whose patients, having apparently been under anaesthetic, can describe in detail the operating theatre, the theatre staff, and what was said during the operation.

Mine occurred in the early seventies. In those days it was best to keep one's counsel to avoid being called a nutter. I had friends who said they could fly about the place at will, but I regarded them with the scepticism that perhaps some people will view me.

One chilly October evening I was walking home, having spent the afternoon in conversation with friend Michael, whom I considered to be a wise man. No drink, no dope, just cups of tea and an intense debate on Christianity. As I left, friend Michael said, 'Dee, you are about to meet yourself – you are ready.' I didn't have a clue what he was on about, but as I wandered along I reflected that, after all my visits to psychiatrists over the years, I knew myself only too well, thank you very much!

The autumn leaves were falling and there were great drifts covering the pavement; a chill wind was blowing and the sky was growing dark. Despite the bleak surroundings I felt warm and happy and a little light headed. What happened next is difficult to explain.

I suddenly realized that I was being given instruction on how to live a righteous life. Did I hear a voice or did the voice come from within myself? I honestly don't know, but I knew I was hearing something very important. I was still trudging along, kicking over the leaves, avoiding lamp posts – in fact behaving quite normally – but I felt detached from my body.

The voice gently reminded me of precepts I knew to be right, but which so often, in the pursuit of emotional, sexual or materialistic fulfilment, I had forgotten about – precepts like honesty, generosity, thoughtfulness, patience, humility, spirituality, in fact all those good qualities that we choose to ignore because they are inconvenient. The one message which did surprise me was that it is wrong to eat meat. This had never been high on my list of priorities when doing a bit of soul searching.

The voice ceased, and something extraordinary occurred. As I turned into the sleazy Earl's Court Road, rain was beginning to drizzle down and the usual assortment of drunks, pimps and junkies were hanging around. It was usually a depressing sight, but not this time: the street was filled with light: great beams were emanating from the people there, my beam intermingling with theirs. There was no elitism: the drunk's light was as strong and sure as that of the 'respectable' people walking by. I stood and watched them; some were chatting, some were reading a paper at the bus stop, some just shuffling about, completely unaware of the goodness and beauty within them.

The expression 'bulls in a china shop' came to mind. If we have the capacity to commune with each other on a spiritual plane (which is how I interpreted the vision before me), then how come we are so blind to it?

I was lucky to experience this loving energy, and I wanted to reach out to the other people around me and share it with them. Good grief, thank goodness I didn't: they would have thought I was just another Earl's Court Road loony. This fear brought me back to myself. The vision slowly evaporated, and my messianic urges with it.

As I turned to walk home my body felt as heavy as that of Il Commendatore when he steps down from the podium at the end of *Don Giovanni*; I could hardly move. It was only then that I realized I had had an out-of-body experience.

The first thing to be done was to cancel my date; I was going to do a rotten thing – go out with the boyfriend of a friend of mine, knowing that she would be hurt if she found out.

Brimming with goodwill towards mankind, I arrived home where my mother had been taking care of the kids. They were screaming at each other as I walked in, but I had the patience of a saint! I felt so much love for them all. I bathed the children and wrapped them in their cosy dressing gowns, and they came and sat by the fire for me to tell them a story. I always loved this time of day – all clean, tantrums over, quietly listening to a magical tale (our favourites were the fairy tales of Oscar Wilde).

Once they were tucked up in bed, I sat down to try and tell my mother what had happened to me, but it soon became obvious that my words were falling on stony ground. She had no concept of what I was talking about, and why should she? These experiences must have occurred since time immemorial, but it wasn't until the sixties that people began to recognize them for what they were – too late for my mother's generation.

I rang Michael and told him. He was delighted for me, but wisely said I should not discuss it with people who weren't ready; it would be wrong to test the fragility of this fresh awareness of mine and have it ridiculed. 'Don't dilute the experience,' he said. 'Keep it strong in your heart.'

Nowadays things are quite different; many people admit to having had similar insights.

I have never experienced this phenomenon again, though I would like to. It would have been especially helpful when I was in the Marsden. But the memory has remained and has brought me great peace. I have tried to incorporate into my life the maxims laid down for me by the voice – with many a lapse – but when I waver over a decision, they serve as my guide.

Jeremy Brett once told me that his mother had died suddenly, and that he was comforted when he managed to contact her through a medium. I had never thought of seeking such a person myself. Then, quite unexpectedly, one found me.

It happened some years before I had cancer: one day the phone rang and it was friend Trisha sounding very pleased with herself. 'Don't worry, Dee,' she said. 'I have found someone who can make our Elvis jacket in forty-eight hours. What a relief, eh?' This was indeed good news for us. We were working together on the wardrobe for a large and complicated commercial. The one thing we could not find was a white buckskin jacket with fringes for our Elvis. Up and down Carnaby Street we had trudged, in vain. The day of the shoot was looming near and we were beginning to panic. 'He's coming to the wardrobe call tonight,' she continued, 'so he can measure our Elvis. He's a useful discovery; I found him in a leather bondage store for gays.'

'What on earth were you doing in such a place?' I asked.

'Look,' said Trisha, 'if he can make us the jacket in such a short time, what does it matter where he comes from? Anyway, be at my flat at seven and we'll take polaroids of all the costumes to see that everyone looks right.'

I arrived in good time to find that the gay bondage man had already taken the measurements of our actor and was on the point of leaving. Trisha introduced us and he looked at me very intensely. 'I knew I had to come here tonight,' he said, 'I had to meet you. Someone in your life has died recently, haven't they?'

I was much taken aback: how could this gay bondage man know anything about me at all? Of course he was right. My mother had died suddenly six weeks before. No illness, no preparation, she just died. She had been taken into hospital for a couple of days with a minor ailment, and when I rang the ward sister she told me that Mum would be out playing tennis again very soon. Perhaps I had a premonition because I asked the sister to ring me, not my father, if anything untoward occurred. Sure enough the phone went at midnight and the sister told me my mother had died five minutes earlier.

It was a great shock, made worse by the fact that Mum had been unhappy during the last years of her life. I felt that she had just turned her face to the wall; she no longer wanted to go on. This feeling of sadness was reflected in her will. She left instructions that no one except me, my brothers and Dad should attend her funeral, not even her brother. This came as a great surprise, for she had always been very gregarious, with loads of friends. It made me realize how lonely she must have been, and I had not been there to help her.

I felt irritated by the gay bondage man (or the GBM, as I shall refer to him) because I had a lot of work to do that evening, and I didn't want to have to humour some fruitcake just because we needed our Elvis jacket.

The GBM took me to one side and seemed to read my thoughts. 'Don't worry,' he said. 'I don't need you now. Just write down the name of the person who has died and I will go into the other room and make notes of what they say.'

I suddenly felt a little scared. I wrote down Mum's name and departed down the long corridor to help Trish dress the actors. I emphasize this in order to make it clear that there was no way that the GBM could use telepathy or anything like that to read my thoughts. I was so busy working and talking that I virtually forgot about him. I remembered reading that Gracie Fields had got through to a medium and had said, 'Ee, 'tis grand on t'other side!' Now I was going to have to be diplomatic and listen to such foolishness in the line of duty.

After about an hour there was a knock on the dressing-room door. It was the GBM saying, 'Deirdre, the force is very strong now, it's time you came with me.' This was fine because we had virtually finished our work and I could relax and see what he had to say. We sat close together on the drawing-room sofa. In his hand the GBM held a sheaf of notes he had made.

He began by talking about my mother's childhood in Ireland. I knew so little about it that he could have said anything he liked really. Then he moved on to her war years, when she ran a hotel for American officers on leave in London. He told me that she had fallen very much in love with someone (I presume with a Yank), as so many women did when their men were away fighting. My father was at sea at the time. This had caused her great anguish and guilt, but her sense of duty finally prevailed: she knew she must stand by her man instead of departing with her new love. According to the GBM, she never got over it.

This was all news to me! I knew absolutely nothing about any such relationship, but the GBM insisted that this had indeed been the case. Later, I checked on this with Mum's closest friend, and he was correct. How could he have known? He couldn't have picked it up from me, because I knew nothing of it. How could he have known unless he was indeed in communication with her?

'I can see her now,' he continued, and described her to me. 'Why is it, Dee, that she only lets me see her on blue water, never on land? She says you will understand.'

Of course I did. My mother had adored life in Malta, especially the summer when we spent wonderful weekends in the Mediterranean on our yacht. She loved the sea, and the boat was her joy.

The GBM confirmed that she had been very unhappy when she died. 'She was a victim in the eternal triangle,' he said. True. My father was involved with another woman, and I don't suppose it matters how old you are: it still hurts.

Then Mum sent some messages that only I could understand; they were to do with our relationship. Feeling a wave of pain, I clutched at the GBM's wrist. His pulse was racing. 'She's going now,' he said, then sat back and breathed deeply for a few minutes.

I had so many questions to ask him that I hardly knew where to start. 'Is she happy now?' was the first one.

'No,' he replied, and my heart sank. 'You see, when you die, you don't just leave behind all the confusion you have helped to create. You have to work your way through it, but she has people with her who are helping her, and she is all right.'

I trusted him then. It would have been so easy for him to say, 'Don't worry your little head, she is just great.' But he didn't, and I respected him for it. He described her two companions – people whom she had known on earth, but I didn't recognize either of them. At least she wasn't lonely.

We sat there in silence, both of us exhausted. Had this really happened, just like that? I didn't know what to think. I asked him why she had talked to me and not to Dad or my brothers. He replied that I must be the only one who had, albeit inadvertently, come across a medium.

The GBM seemed a kind, gentle man, so I asked him why, if he was so damn bright, he made leather bondage gear – hardly an enlightened pursuit, I thought. He smiled and replied enigmatically, 'It's what I enjoy this time round.' Well, I was not going to pursue that one and get into a debate on reincarnation; I had enough to occupy my mind.

He got up to leave and gave me his card, urging me to ring him if I ever had need of him again. I stood up to say goodbye and he hugged me. 'Don't worry,' he said, and left.

Now, he didn't ask me for money, he certainly was not after my body, he said he knew that he *had* to come to Trisha's (and not just to fit our Elvis). What should I make of it all? I don't know. I told Trisha what had happened and she too was completely astonished.

I got back home feeling quite staggered. I needed to talk to someone who could help me see the episode in perspective. Friend Mark was there and we pondered on how the GBM could have known so much.

Mark's reaction to the story was very down-to-earth. 'Did you check out the pub situation up there?' he asked.

'No,' I answered crossly. 'It would have seemed trivial in the extreme.'

'You silly cow,' friend Mark went on. 'What a lost opportunity to set everyone's mind at rest about that one.'

I thought it best not to say a word to Dad about all this, but I did try to talk to my brothers. They didn't want to hear it. They were both grieving, and perhaps they found such information upsetting and alarming.

Did Mum really come through? Had she really contacted me? Who can say? I spent some time thinking, talking to people who had experienced this phenomenon, reading books about it (especially those by Michael Bentine), and I became convinced that she did. It was a great comfort to me, as it had been to Jeremy Brett, and it formed yet another stepping stone in my changing perception of death.

If you feel you would like to contact a medium, make sure that you find a reputable one, either by recommendation or by ringing the Spiritualists' National Union (01279 81620 – they have a register of bona fide mediums in all parts of the country), or the Spiritualist Association of Great Britain (0171 235 3351).

My first experience of acupuncture came when I was struck down with a bad back. I had never suffered from back pain, and was not very sympathetic to friends who would roll about in agony on the floor, moaning and groaning. I assumed that there was a touch of exaggeration going on. How mistaken I had been.

I awoke one morning, scarcely able to move without incurring appalling pain. I couldn't think what was wrong with me – it clearly was not a side effect of my radiotherapy treatment. After wriggling about for some time, trying to inch my way along without aggravating the stabbing pain in my back, I managed to hobble awkwardly to the bathroom. By now I was in tears.

Friend Robin was about as sympathetic as I had been to my friends. 'What on earth is the matter now?' he asked. Poor Robin, he had already been witness to my bad bouts of sickness on chemotherapy, but he soon realized that this was no faking for attention; it was serious.

I live a stone's throw from the new Chelsea and Westminster Hospital, so Robin and I decided that it would be best to try and make it to the emergency department. Somehow I got some clothes on and, very slowly and painfully, made my way to the hospital. After waiting for what seemed an inordinate length of time, I was seen by a young doctor who examined me thoroughly. 'I can find nothing wrong with you,' he said. 'It might be a trapped nerve. We will have to wait and see how you get on. However,' he continued, 'with your medical history it might be wise, if the pain doesn't go away, to be checked at the Marsden. Bone cancer can sometimes follow breast cancer, so it's best to be sure.' Well, this was news to me. Bad news. 'Just lie as flat as you can on the floor for about three weeks, and I'm sure it will go away,' he added.

'But I can't stand this pain, certainly not for three weeks! Surely there must be something you can do!' I wailed.

'I'll write out a prescription for some painkillers,' was his reply.

'Do you not think that I might try a chiropractor?' I asked him.

'Oh, don't waste your time with that new-fangled rubbish,' he said. 'Just do as I say and you'll be fine.'

Robin went and got the pills for me, and I hobbled back home, clutching on to him, hardly able to move without searing spasms piercing my lower back. Once home, I lay flat on the floor as instructed and waited for the painkillers to take effect. The phone rang and it was Jemma. I was crying as I spoke to her and explained what had happened. 'I'm coming straight over to pick you up and take you to my acupuncturist,' she said. It sounded like a nightmare – being jolted all the way to Kentish Town in her Beetle was more than I could take, but she was insistent and would brook no argument.

Having heard the doctor's opinions on 'new-fangled nonsense', I was dubious about an instant cure. I felt perhaps I was better off on the floor. However, Jemma soon arrived and she and Robin helped to get me into her car – sheer agony! Every time she changed gear I nearly went through the roof! Eventually we arrived at a holistic healing centre, and

Jemma helped me into the waiting room, promising that acupuncture would work wonders. It was so kind of her to take the trouble to drive across London to fetch me that I attempted to smile at her, but it was difficult.

After a short wait I was shown into the surgery where the acupuncturist gave my back a thorough checking. He then inserted several needles into my back, which didn't hurt at all, and left me alone, saying he would return in twenty minutes to twiddle them. Having done this, he left for another twenty minutes. I lay there, trying to relax my muscles as best I could. Then back he came again. 'We're finished,' he said. 'You can go home now.'

I began to stand up as gingerly as I had all day, but there was no pain. The clinic only asked for a donation that I could afford.

It was a remarkable result. I walked with Jemma back to her car, my senses on red alert for any twinges, but there were none. I persuaded her to drop me at a bus stop to save her battling her way to Chelsea in rush-hour traffic and sat nervously on the bus, wondering if this cure would last until I got home. This was the real test, for the bus driver drove as if he were on speed, roaring along then braking so hard that the passengers standing up were in danger of their lives.

At home I was hardly able to believe that I was free from the morning agony. The acupuncturist had warned me that I might need one more session, but I was fine. I never had another back spasm.

A friend of mine went to an acupuncturist – or so he called himself - who kept diagnosing all kinds of fictitious ailments which needed treatment. It soon came clear that all this twiddling of needles made her desire him. He was manipulating her into his bed! So be careful when choosing your acupuncturist!

I very much wanted to ring the young doctor I had seen in the Chelsea and Westminster Emergency Department who had displayed such ignorance of alternative healing, but I didn't know his name. He would have had me on my back in agony for weeks, yet here I was, fit again and able to function quite normally. Doctors, please take note.

Acupuncture can cure a wide variety of ailments: migraine, skin disorders . . . the list is endless. If something is worrying you, ring either of these two main numbers for general information and to find your nearest practitioner: The Acupuncture Foundation (0171 490 0721) or The Council for Acupuncture (0171 121 5756).

My first foray into the world of alternative healing was a great surprise to me. I had assumed that it was something that took place at Lourdes, or at huge rallies presided over by a megalomaniac who exhorted the sick to throw away their sticks and walk. How ignorant I was to have completely missed out on the rich, diverse and inspirational range of holistic healing.

Jemma and I set off for the country one beautiful summer's day to see a famous healer who had been highly recommended to us. I was still on chemotherapy at this time, and although I trusted orthodox medicine, it seemed sensible to try everything I could to get rid of the cancer. I felt rather nervous – I half expected someone in a gypsy scarf, a pack of tarot cards on the table with Death facing upwards, and a crystal ball which might well show *bad news*!

Nothing could have been further from the truth. We arrived at a charming country house to be met by a smart elderly woman who welcomed us into her drawing room. Looking around, I could see that she must be a very successful healer because a lot of money had gone into that room. She had already explained to us that the treatment would take all day, and that she would provide lunch.

We all sat down and started exchanging pleasantries when she suddenly got up and walked over to a formidable drinks cabinet from which she pulled a large bottle of Smirnoff and some tonic saying, 'I never work on anyone unless they have had some vodka.'

Jemma looked aghast, but it was music to my ears and my nerves vanished in a trice. 'You may smoke if you wish,' she added, so then I really felt at home.

She poured me a stiff vodka and an equally stiff one for herself, and we settled on the sofa to start the healing. This was all a million miles from what I had imagined – there was vodka and fags and not a tarot card in sight. I settled back to enjoy my treatment, congratulating myself on my choice of healer; she was the very one for me!

She asked me how I was feeling, and a picture of my mother slipped into my mind ('Darling, never ask anyone how they are because they might tell you!'). I explained that I was not in pain, but was on chemotherapy, which I found very hard to take. 'When you leave here,' said the healer, 'your days on chemotherapy will be over.' How I prayed she would be right.

She sat close to me and placed her hand over the malignant breast, making plucking movements for so long that I thought her arm must surely drop off. While she was doing this she intoned prayers to God, whom she called 'Papa'. Occasionally with her other hand she had a sip of vodka. I was confused about her drinking because my 'Attitude Squad' friends all said that drinking removed one from one's spiritual being. Still, if you think about all the monks creating fine liqueurs such as Cointreau and Commanderie St John, why should this be the case?

When we adjourned for lunch Jemma and I heard about people with a huge range of ailments whom she had healed. She had also been called in to heal animals, including fine thoroughbred horses – National or Derby contenders which were off colour. She had piles of press cuttings to support her claims, which made me feel excited about my cure.

After lunch she resumed her seat on the sofa close to me, and carried on making plucking and massaging motions over my breast for what seemed like hours. She stopped abruptly, had a chat with 'Papa' and pronounced me cured. 'You will find that the malignancy has gone, my dear, before you are due for your next bout of chemotherapy. Ask the doctor for a biopsy, and he will confirm what I have said, that you are just fine.'

I was overjoyed. I felt as if a great weight had been taken from me. All I had to do now was check with the Marsden and I would be free – free to start my life again. *Oh, thank you, healer; oh, thank you, God.*

Before we departed Jemma kindly paid the £100 fee. Living on Sickness Benefit, I just couldn't afford it.

As we drove back to London I looked around at the lovely Hampshire countryside. Great may trees covered in creamy blossom were dotted in the green fields of grazing cattle. I saw such harmony in those lush pastures, such calm, such stillness. It had been so long since I had been out of London that I had forgotten the joy to be found away from our urban nightmare, the delight of rolling meadows. Tears rolled down my cheeks at the beauty of these forgotten scenes, and with the relief of knowing that I was cured.

One week later, I arrived at the Marsden for my next chemotherapy injection. I explained to the consultant that I had been to see a healer who had pronounced me clear of cancer and asked him for a biopsy before I had my injection. I did wonder if he might think I was mad, but he was happy to comply. I was pleased to find that alternative therapies are being accepted by more and more orthodox doctors.

The results came back and my malignancy was still there. *Large as life*. Nothing had changed. I was devastated and all my fear returned – the old churning stomach while queueing with the other unfortunates for my fix. What had gone wrong?

The visit had augured so well, but I still had to go on with the endless chemotherapy.

It occurred to me that since the healer was so successful, I had not been cured because there was something wrong with me. Typical me: blame yourself, blame yourself! But she had even cured horses, for heaven's sake! Where did that leave me? Furthermore, neither I nor Jemma could afford another session. The poor die first.

I am sounding a bit disgruntled here, but I don't mean to be. The healer was full of wisdom and kindness, and I know of many people she has successfully cured, although it didn't work for me that time.

Some months later, shortly after I had finished my course of radiotherapy, my old friend Eva rang me. She told me that she had become a healer and, having just heard that I had cancer, she suggested we meet up to see if I would like a course of healing sessions with her. Thus began my second foray into the world of alternative healing.

The call surprised me considerably because I remembered Eva as a beautiful, successful scriptwriter. One of her scripts was for the film *She'll Be Wearing Pink Pyjamas*, starring Julie Walters, which I had enjoyed very much.

I knew that Eva had also been a Fleet Street journalist. A woman who dealt in hard facts. Yet here she was, telling me that she was a healer.

After my first experience of healing I was naturally cautious about getting my hopes up. However, I cast my doubts aside and duly arrived at her front door a few days later, filled, if not with faith, at least with curiosity.

She lived in a quiet residential street, where all the houses looked the same – except hers, which was painted yellow, with a white front door and a large magnolia tree in the front garden. As my visits became regular, I came to see this tree as a beacon of light in the grey conformity of the neighbourhood. It reminded me of childhood fairy tales about some poor weary traveller, lost in a dark wood, suddenly filled with hope at the sight of a bright cottage window beckoning through the trees.

I was immediately struck by the atmosphere of serenity in the house. Eva was as beautiful and warm as ever, and as I followed her into the kitchen I was glad that I had come. We sat and talked over cups of tea, and I was relieved to discover that she still smoked. With all the boring political correctness there is about nowadays, sometimes you feel as if you are committing a criminal offence when you light up, and I had imagined that she might well be part of the 'Attitude Squad' now!

After a while she suggested that we go upstairs for my first healing session. She asked me to lie down on the large cream-coloured waterbed, explaining that being near water is helpful in healing. Jung, I recalled, had also advised people to live near water because it nourishes the soul, but I had always thought this somewhat elitist – I mean, what would happen if the whole of Birmingham downed tools and headed for the coast?

Eva told me: 'Now you may experience various sensations: perhaps the symptoms of your current illness or former illnesses will intensify. Don't worry about it. They will just pass away. In fact, don't worry about anything that happens or doesn't happen. Just shut your eyes and breathe out. You may find yourself falling asleep. If you do, just let yourself.'

I lay there wondering what was she doing. I did try to keep my eyes shut but curiosity got the better of me! I saw her hands moving over me, their movements so graceful that they reminded me of an Indian dancer's. Sometimes they moved slowly, sometimes quickly, with many delicate finger movements. After a while my eyes must have closed. When I opened them again, Eva was still sitting behind me, perfectly still.

'Are you back?' she asked.

Back? What did she mean? Where did she think I'd been? My eyes happened to focus on a clock. I had been lying on the bed for four hours! *Four hours!* I realized I had lost all sense of time. I didn't know whether I had been lying there for ten minutes or two days. Yet I had no memory of actually falling asleep or waking up. The whole process had been so gentle.

'Would you like to come and have another cup of tea?' said Eva. As I followed her downstairs, I realized I felt deeply refreshed and relaxed, as though I'd woken from the deepest sleep of my life.

'You probably have,' said Eva. 'It's a state very similar to deep meditation. Your brainwaves slow down. I call it going into your own personal sanctuary. People are put in touch with their own curative powers.'

I remembered then that I had personally experienced a similar feeling of love and peace in my out-of-body experience.

One day I asked Eva how she had become a healer. She laughed. 'If anyone had told me ten years ago that they were a healer, I would have thought that they were nuts. But now I realize that meeting two healers when I did, one after the other, and receiving healing from them was the beginning of the most important journey of my life – the spiritual journey. Or perhaps I should say, it led to my recognizing that the spiritual journey is the real one. We are all on that journey, it's impossible not to be, we're not necessarily aware of it.

'It wasn't just that these healers achieved results for my physical health where orthodox medicine had failed. In retrospect, to me their importance is that they began the opening of doors in my mind.

'Deirdre, until then I was so cynical about anything to do

124

with this area, in my mind the door wasn't just shut, it was locked and the key was buried. But what these two healers did *worked* and I had to take notice. Until then I'd say that by a lot of people's standards I'd led an interesting adventurous life. But the real adventure only began once I became conscious of the spiritual road. I highly recommend it to everyone.'

Within a few months Eva received a telephone call from a friend in India inviting her to stay. 'I accepted straight away which in itself was a most unusual thing to do,' said Eva. 'But by that time I was getting the hang of what you might call "going with the flow."' And it was there, in India, that Eva first put her hands over someone's head – and discovered that she was a healer.

'When people come to me they usually have illnesses which allopathic medicine has been unable to help,' she said. 'By the time they get to me, they've usually tried everything else. They've been living with their back pain or whatever for years. I'm usually a last resort.

'I wasn't surprised to learn recently that many doctors and nurses are training as healers. They're already "naturals", people who have chosen a caring profession.

'All you need to discover is what healers the world over know – that love is the most powerful thing in the universe. It is behind every religion in the world.'

So my weekly healings continued. I had begun by taking a bunch of flowers, calling it my Buddhist offering! But after a few weeks my Buddhist offering became a shepherd's pie! I could see that after some sessions Eva was very tired. She was healing people every day. I thought that cooking was probably the last thing she felt like afterwards.

During one healing session I saw the colour blue – deep, iridescent blue. Eva explained to me that people often did see colours, always beautiful and always like no colour they have ever seen. They also often feel deep heat, and find themselves back in a real-life experience – a traumatic incident perhaps. But then something calms them and they release their pain, fear and grief and experience the power of healing love.

As I write this, I'm more that aware that it sounds . . . corny. But I know that I experienced that state – a feeling of absolute peace.

One day before our healing session, Eva received a phone call. It was from another woman who had had breast cancer for the second time and had come to Eva for healing.

She was phoning now to say that her mammogram had come through and she was clear. She no longer had cancer. 'The consultant even said that in his opinion healers could not be over-estimated!' Eva told me afterwards, exuding joy.

Eva had been transformed into this spiritual being, and I wanted to know whether everyone has this potential within them.

She told me that she believed 'transformation' or 'evolvement' was the point of human existence. That we can transform ourselves now, in this life.

She showed me a room in her house full of beautiful paintings. I had not and still have not seen anything like them – they all had an extraordinarily soothing effect, exuding balance, harmony and joy. I was amazed to discover that Eva had painted them. To me these paintings seemed nothing less than sacred art.

'These are tangible examples of what can happen when the door in the mind is opened,' she told me. 'I paint from a place of peace within myself in the same way that I heal. I believe that receiving healing is a way of opening ourselves to a flow of creative energy – a way of allowing the soul to speak. You need to spend time every day "listening to your soul". It likes to be given time. Stop and really listen to that piece of music, really look at that painting. Deliberately and consciously look for something that you love doing so much that if you were offered money not to do it, you'd refuse. Put your heart and soul into what you do – even simple everyday tasks.

'I think most creative people have experienced those times when the thing they are working on seems to be creating itself. That's when inspiration, the creative flow of the universe is there. People accept inspiration in all the arts, and healing is an inspired art.'

Eva seemed to me to have found so many ways of expressing her soul. As my weekly visits to her continued I realized that she was not just my friend and healer, she was my spiritual teacher. Often I would call her in the evenings when I felt low and she was always there for me.

My healing sessions began to take less time and one day, a week before I was due for a biopsy at the Marsden, I was there for only forty-five minutes. Eva telephoned me the evening before my appointment. 'Fingers and toes crossed,' she said.

I lay in my hospital cubicle, waiting for the result of my biopsy. *Tick, tock, tick, tock, tick, tock.* Cut to a shot of the clock, Mr Hitchcock, please. How many other poor women were lying in the matching cubicles waiting for a reprieve? *Tick tock, tick tock.* The time between the *tick* and the *tock* was getting longer. I knew it was. Surely I was now rid of this loathsome disease. I'd had all that chemotherapy and radiotherapy. I'd received six months of healing. Surely, if it had been getting any worse they would have done something. No, I mustn't get too excited. I mustn't hope too much. I had to stay balanced so as not to be devastated if the result was negative.

Tick, tock. Tick, tock. Tick, tock. I concentrated hard at visualizing the lump being transformed into a white mist, evaporating in a breeze. At least I was doing something positive.

Tick, tock. Tick, tock. The door of my cubicle opened. The young doctor stood there. He was smiling. 'You're OK, Deirdre,' he said.

I know I just stared at him. The sense of euphoria I was expecting never came. I seemed just as unable to absorb the fact that I was healed as I had to absorb the fact that I had cancer.

The doctor went on, 'You still have a few cancer cells but they are dying. There's nothing to worry about.'

Nothing to worry about! I had nothing to worry about any more. One minute you are seriously, possibly mortally ill, the next you're healed, 'just like that'.

I was now in remission. This meant that I had to return to the Marsden every three months for a check-up and I was taking Tamoxifen, an anti-oestrogen drug that has proved very effective in the treatment of breast cancer.

I wandered home from the Marsden trying to feel something, but I had buttoned up my emotions for so long now that I couldn't react any more. I thought back to that first time I had walked home from the Marsden. It felt like eons ago. I wanted to be able to weep with relief, but I could not weep. Even when my brother Rob had committed suicide I could not weep. Yet I had always been such a cry baby. Show me a movie, show me a sunset, and I was away. Not any more. I had not cried for two and a half years - ever since I discovered I had cancer.

I rang around family and friends to tell them my news and they were ecstatic. It was very therapeutic to hear other people's joy, to experience it even at second hand.

I rang Eva. She, too, was overjoyed. 'Can I still come and see you next week?' I asked. 'Just for a cup of tea?' Looking back, I think I was like a child clinging on to a blanket. When I got home after seeing Eva I cried and cried for the first time. It was such a relief!

Penny Brohn, that brave campaigner for holistic cures and co-founder of the Bristol Cancer Help Centre, writes at the end of her book, *Gentle Giants*: '. . . if having cancer is the way to "open now the crystal fountain whence the healing stream doth flow", then it's no bad thing.'

I would like to end this chapter on complementary medicine by quoting from an article that appeared in the *Nursing Times* – an eminently respectable source – on 2 November 1994:

> There are 6200 healers who are members of the major UK organizations. In 155 controlled studies it has been shown that healing can have significant effects on humans, animals, plants, bacteria, yeasts, cells in vitro, enzymes, and so on.
>
> Healing has been proven to be of significant help in conditions for which conventional treatments have limited results such as arthritis, chronic fatigue syndrome, multiple sclerosis, cancer, cardiovascular problems, diabetes mellitus, pain, anxiety, wound healing, blood pressure and haemoglobin levels.
>
> Healing is safe and has no know deleterious side-effects, although pain occasionally increases in initial treatments.
>
> Ninety per cent of doctors and nurses who register for healing training in courses or workshops find that they have some measure of healing ability.

If you would like to find a healer near you, I suggest you try:

The Institute of Complementary Medicine (0171 237 5165)
The Confederation of Healing Organizations (01442 870667)
The National Federation of Healers (01891 616080).

7
Reflection and Rebirth

> . . . to me alone there came a thought of grief:
> A timely utterance gave that thought relief.
> And I again am strong . . .
> – *William Wordsworth*

A few years ago designer Geoff Sharpe asked me to be his wardrobe assistant on the film of *Echoes*, which was to be shot in Ireland. Friend Barbara Rennie had adapted it for the screen from the novel by Maeve Binchy and was to direct it, and friend Geraldine James was to star in it. I was delighted. Although both my parents came from Ireland, I had never been there, and had always wanted to go. This was the perfect opportunity.

It was an extraordinary experience. This might sound like Celtic blarney, but the minute I set foot on the soil I knew I had come home at last. I cherished every moment I was there, despite the hard work: the wardrobe department started every morning at four-thirty, sometimes working through until midnight. There is a saying in Hollywood: 'The wardrobe people die first!' but if I had died on that shoot I would have died happy!

The overwhelmingly poetic beauty of the landscape in those early autumn days filled me with joy. The air that I breathed seemed charmed with creative energy. Even the statues of the Blessed Virgin in little roadside grottoes, which the crew joked about, I found touching, not mawkish.

At our main location there was a little ten-year-old boy called Finnigan, who followed me about like a puppy. 'Now be sure, Deadra, that you get me a part in the fillum tomorrow,' he would demand. One evening he was sitting next to me on a bench as I supervised the costume during a night shoot and we got talking about travel. I asked where he would like to go. 'Japan,' he replied.

'Why?' I asked him.

He looked at me as if I were a moron. 'Well, Deadra,' he said, ''cos they told me it is indeed part of Paradise.'

Only an Irish child could have said something so beautiful in all true faith and innocence. I wanted to pack him in my suitcase and take him home with me. I loved the Irish people; I shared with them my broad face, red hair and freckles. My name had become 'Deadra' – so much more lilting than Deirdre, which I had always hated; now I was proud that I was named after an early Celtic queen.

It is quite a revelation when, late in life, you stumble across your true national identity. Of course, I had never felt English either – I had been brought up in the Mediterranean and had felt closer to those peoples. But this was the real thing; this was home. Why was it that I had always thought in some brainwashed way that Ireland belonged to Edna O'Brien? Well, it didn't! Now *I* had my foot in the door.

I cried when it was time for me to leave and resolved that one day I would find the means to own a cottage there. 'The pipes, the pipes were calling,' and they still are.

By the end of the eighties work had all but dried up for me on the films and commercials front, so finding myself in my customary financial dire straits I sat down and wrote a Mills and Boon novel with my sights firmly set on the cottage in Ireland. It really was fun and, full of confidence, I sent *Malta Passion* off to the publishers.

They were very nice about it but said that the conflict

between the hero and heroine was not sufficiently intense; however, they would like me to write for them – why didn't I start work again on another story? Well, since our hero had kidnapped our heroine, had raped her and blackmailed her into becoming his mistress, it was difficult to see how much more intense things could have got! The thought of starting all over again was a bit daunting so I decided to give it a rest for a while.

In the spring of 1991, before I knew I had cancer, I was fifty-two and, like my contemporaries, doing my best to come to terms with bad news. Friend Sue had gone on holiday to Rome and came back in a state of shock because for the first time she had been addressed as '*Signora!*' 'There's always something there to remind you,' sang Sandie. How right she was!

Perhaps those of us who sang along with The Who, 'Hope I die before I get old,' were now beginning to regret the youthful challenge thrown down so wilfully; those of us who mourned the passing of the Leader of the Pack felt uneasily that we might soon be joining him in the Ace Café in the sky.

It wasn't so much intimations of mortality that worried me then – I hadn't come to that one yet; but I didn't know how to face middle and old age with equanimity. There is a marvellous poem by Jenny Joseph on ageing that goes as follows:

Warning

When I am an old woman I shall wear purple
With a red hat that doesn't go, and doesn't suit me,
And I shall spend my pension on brandy and summer gloves
And satin sandals, and say we've no money for butter.
I shall sit down on the pavement when I'm tired
And gobble up samples in shops and press alarm bells
And run my stick along the public railings
And make up for the sobriety of my youth.
I shall go out in my slippers in the rain
And pick the flowers in other people's gardens
And learn to spit.

You can wear terrible shirts and grow more fat
And eat three pounds of sausages at a go
Or only bread and pickle for a week
And hoard pens and pencils and beer mats and things in boxes.

But now we must have clothes that keep us dry
And pay our rent and not swear in the street
And set a good example for the children.
We must have friends to dinner and read the papers.

But maybe I ought to practise a little now?
So people who know me are not too shocked and surprised
When suddenly I am old, and start to wear purple.

I love that poem; I have indulged myself in all her images of anarchy except for learning to spit! I would shock no one! Equanimity, I had discovered, was the name of my game.

As I reviewed my life, my thoughts had turned to Jemma and Luke. They had long left home and were both doing well in their chosen professions. Giving up nurturing and feeling needed was hard, but my fine cat, Captain, had helped. I had long anticipated this stage in my life: I was well prepared to take a back seat in my children's lives.

When they were tiny, I had been much inspired by a quote from *The Prophet* by Kahlil Gibran:

Your children are not your children.
They are the sons and daughters of Life's longing for itself.
They come through you but not from you.
And though they are with you yet they belong not to you.
You may give them your love but not your thoughts.
For they have their own thoughts.
You may house their bodies but not their souls,
For their souls dwell in the house of tomorrow,
which you cannot visit, not even in your dreams.
You may strive to be like them, but seek not to make them like
   you . . .

What a change from the Thought Police who ruled my childhood. 'You are the bows from which your children as living arrows are sent forth.' Now the arrows had gone forth, and the old bow had to find itself a new identity, to re-invent itself in some way.

I had never been that hot on finding an integrated identity for myself. It was that old problem of whether to be the Madonna or Mary Magdalene? The virgin or the whore? 'Honky Tonk Woman' beckoned alluringly on one side, purity and peace of mind on the other. We ex-convent girls have a lot of trouble with that one.

Back in the sixties my psychiatrist had asked me to write an essay on my childhood role models. Talk about a split personality! On one side there was Beatrix Potter's Mrs Rabbit, nurturing all her baby rabbits in their charming little burrow beneath the great fir-tree. She would tuck them into their little cots, and make them camomile tea to drink out of little blue-and-white china cups. She was forever bustling about, caring and succouring in her selfless way. Vying with this was the image of Maureen O'Hara tossing her long red hair and swashbuckling her way in *The Spanish Main*, and capturing the heart of the handsome bold pirate, Paul Henreid.

Can you see fine Mrs Rabbit, with only fur to toss, no sword in her paw, capturing the heart of the pirate? Or Maureen content in the little burrow, without a man in sight?

My little rabbits had long since scampered away into the meadows, and I was too old to be Maureen, anyway. I had played her for so long I was bored of her, so who could I be?

Even at the age of fourteen, when I had just arrived at my convent in France, I was aware of this mind—body split. Every day I had an hour of French conversation with a wise old nun, who once said to me, 'Deirdre, I have never before met a child who on the one hand has such a thirst for spiritual growth, and on the other such an appetite for excitement, for love of life.'

At fourteen this bothered me not a jot. However, when in later years I found myself havering at a crossroads I would think back to the wise old nun's insight and it helped me to find a perspective.

As I looked back over my life I was well aware that I had had more than my fair share of romance, passion, love, laughter and adventure. It wasn't a question of wishing things had been different (the only thing I might conceivably have wished for was the cushion of a reasonable income); no, I just felt on a Highway to Nowhere. I was drifting. I love working very hard as long as someone pushes me in the right direction and tells me what to do. I have always been hopeless at self-motivation.

So I drifted. I awoke each morning with an uneasy sense of universal angst, something you never experience when you are working on a project or bringing up children – when there is some shape, some point, some discipline in your day. Much of my time was spent on the phone. Panicking girlfriends would ring. Major themes were: 'Dee, I just don't know how to handle living on my own without a man'; or 'Dee, I can't stand living with X, Y, or Z any more, but I'm scared of a divorce.' Some spent their time answering lonely heart ads. None of these worries preoccupied me; I had long lived on my own and had learnt not to rely on men. 'If one comes along, then fine,' I thought. 'If one doesn't come along, I'll deal with that later.'

My feeling of unease was much less specific. I could not shake off a feeling of disquiet, of vexation of the spirit. I was looking at the future through a fog of apprehension which, try as I might, I could not rationalize away. Little did I realize that a massive lesson in living was on its way to really sort me out, once and for all – cancer.

This will sound preposterous to anyone starting out on the

grim journey. In that spring of 1991, I had panicked; I had felt terrified, lost and lonely. I too would have found the idea preposterous at that time. How could I possibly have had an inkling of the good to be found in amidst the nightmare? How could I have anticipated the way in which my life would be enhanced? Or the great wave of love and support that surged towards me from friends and strangers alike? For in that land of the sick I discovered compassion, forbearance, sympathy and approbation – qualities that transformed my self-image and taught me to trust in myself – in my courage to fight and in my ability to find my own way.

I included in this book the chapter on 'My Life Pre Cancer' not as mere self-indulgence, but because in order to understand why people have certain strengths, one must first know them. Everyone should be able to unlock their formative experiences and draw strength from them when they are confronted by trauma and illness. We can be so daunted by the bad news that we forget the resolve we have mustered along the way in dealing with all sorts of problems and crises.

The words 'cancer' and 'victim' are inextricably linked. I took a long look at my life and realized I was *not* a victim; nor would I even entertain the idea of becoming one. Take a look at your life, and appreciate all the battles you have previously won, however insignificant they may seem, and draw on your past strengths, the better to fight this battle for your future.

It is impossible to quantify the lessons that I have learnt over the last three years. The inspirational counsel I received has enhanced my life and opened my eyes to the radiance and splendour of Universal Love and Inner Wisdom.

Katherine Mansfield wrote: 'We have to find the gift in suffering . . . we can't afford to waste such an expenditure of feeling, we have to learn from it.' I learnt that it is all important to find the right attitude for yourself. From the death of your first gerbil, you discover loss and suffering. But how you deal with that loss is what counts. One person perceives illness as retribution, another as a test; it's obvious who is going to cope better.

When I was ill I had plenty of time to meditate, read, absorb fresh information, listen to my inner voice – in effect to restructure my whole vision of life. I used that time well. Instead of my usual dabbling with ideas and philosophies, I embraced all wisdom. Now I found that I was free of the half-baked notions over which I had once agonized and my perception of death was completely transformed. I had found a firm platform and could now face the rest of my life. What a wonderful metamorphosis!

A friend in America who developed breast cancer told me that over there, it is almost like being a criminal. 'Hey, you brought this stuff on yourself,' goes the psychobabble. The Great American Dream of the perfect bosom is threatened by any lumps – except those containing silicone, of course.

The terror that the word 'cancer' conjures up was perfectly illustrated to me when I sent a synopsis of this book to a top literary agent. He wrote back a charming and encouraging letter, but said that he could not take it on because of his phobia about the word. He had also rejected Jill Ireland's fine book, *Life Wish*.

Something must be done to demystify the word. It is viewed with much the same superstition and dread as leprosy was in the Middle Ages. You can't open a newspaper nowadays without reading about some poor person who has succumbed to it – but what about the millions who have recovered? Where are they? Are success stories too boring? – 'Mrs Smith of Hounslow has successfully recovered from cancer after treatment and is happily resuming her life . . .'!

But there are myriad other terrible diseases which, while

they are regarded with fear, do not have the same stigma attached. Why is this so?

I mentioned earlier friend Penny, who has been in a wheelchair for five years as a result of multiple sclerosis. We had known each other since early childhood in Malta and had remained close ever since. Like many of our generation in the late fifties we were rebels and, having turned down some boring invitation to a Debs' ball, we would aim for Soho in great excitement, heading for Cy Laurie's Jazz Club, the Mecca for all traditional jazz fans. We became expert jivers and appeared on *The Six Five Special*, the precursor to *Ready, Steady, Go*, doing an exhibition jive. This particular *Six Five Special* was embarrassingly subtitled 'Here Come the Debs', but as long as the music and our partners were good, we didn't care.

We were also selected by a TV crew who saw us twisting in Chelsea's Café des Artistes to appear in the *Hey, Let's Twist* contest, which was being shot the following week. We arrived with our partners in great excitement, thinking that this might be our chance to be 'discovered' by a dance talent scout – in those days they were all over town like a rash.

The Master of Ceremonies explained to the 200 or so hopeful contestants that when the music started we should start twisting, then, if one of the celebrity panel of judges tapped us on the shoulder we were out. No appeal, just out!

We went to the dance floor and stood waiting until the voice of Chubby Checker started us off. I had just stretched one leg out in front of me and leant back to start twisting when I felt a tap on my shoulder. I was outraged! I turned round and there was Danny Blanchflower smiling at me. This was no smiling matter! *Danny Blanchflower!* What on earth did he know about dancing? Clearly zilch! I hated him for taking away my big chance. There I was, ruined by some lunatic footballer, and I wished own goals on him for the rest of his life!

Penny and I had cried together the first time I saw her in a wheelchair, and we had cried when I told her I had cancer, and yet it seemed just like yesterday that we were the archetypal fifties teenagers, jiving and rocking to Elvis with no care for the future. We drew great mutual support from the length and commitment of our friendship, and whatever happened, at least we knew we had enjoyed marvellous times together.

I doubt very much that I could have resigned myself to Penny's situation with her patience and lack of bitterness. 'It's like serving a prison sentence with no time off for Good Behaviour,' she observes wryly but, now that she has invested in an electric wheelchair, she gets great pleasure from being able to shop unescorted in her local supermarket and tending her garden on her own – things that we take for granted or regard as a chore. I have learned from her that when fate shifts the goalposts you simply carry on playing within the confines of new rules.

While doing research for this book I came across story after story of women who, if a breast lump had been properly diagnosed, would have had every chance of recovery. If you discover a lump, demand a mammogram just to set your mind at rest – whatever your GP says. It is your right! My generation was brought up to view doctors with awe and respect, a bit like a god really. We tend to think they know everything. They *don't*! Moreover, because of the NHS cutbacks, we are reluctant to take up their time. Remember that you are paying for this service; don't put off that appointment.

If your biopsy proves to be malignant, my advice is to buy a copy of *Love, Medicine and Miracles* by Dr Bernie Siegel. I keep mentioning this book because I cannot stress strongly enough how much it helped me to find a positive attitude to fighting cancer.

I find myself compelled to learn from other people's experiences of facing death. Recently I stayed up late watching a film on TV called *Fatal Love* – the true story of a young woman who contracts Aids from a one-night stand. When told that she is HIV positive, the young woman simply falls apart. No one – neither her family nor her counsellors – could help her in this crisis. Then, in an Aids clinic she met a young man who was dying. He told her about a book that had helped him to come to terms with his illness and gave it to her. It was . . . *Love, Medicine and Miracles*! She not only read it but started to attend Bernie Siegel's group meetings – my hero was there on the screen. The young woman is now very successful and lectures on Aids all over the world. The book transformed her life as it did mine.

Your next task is to find out how reliable your family and friends are in giving you support. Friend Ruby discovered that her husband was having an affair with the woman next door the same week she discovered she had breast cancer. She was utterly devastated. And when she turned to family and friends for comfort, they were so horrified that they simply refused to discuss her illness. There she was, her marriage to a man she still loved breaking up, abandoned by everybody, utterly alone in this crisis. I cannot imagine the suffering that she went through but, being the brave, positive woman that she is, she began what she describes as an 'inner journey'. She joined a cancer support group, made new friends, and recognized, as I did, the importance of *growing* through this experience.

If you feel lonely and isolated, and would like to join a cancer support group, you can usually get information on local groups through your hospital. If not, CancerLink (0171 833 2451) lists support groups all over the country. I am now part of that organization, and befriend people who are going through the same trauma that I did. I say 'befriend' because I find the word 'counsellor' a little pompous. It implies that you are in a superior position. Not so. I learn from these women just as they learn from me. Also, if you have family or friends who have cancer and you are finding it hard to cope, ring CancerLink and they will advise you on where to find support. I cannot recommend them too highly.

You might be surprised to discover that some people you thought you could rely on turn out to be fair-weather friends. It happened to me. I am more circumspect about friendships now. I am not naturally cautious where emotions are concerned, but I try not to be so trusting. On the other hand, you can find that people you only thought of as acquaintances come through magnificently; a transitory relationship becomes a true friendship. Thanks, Anya!

These past few years have been my Odyssey, my journey into uncharted waters. Here I have discovered a new world of hope, love, and beauty. I can truthfully say I would not change a thing.

I am a very fortunate woman and cannot sufficiently express my gratitude to all those who have helped me along the way, especially my beloved children, Jemma and Luke. I also have the joy of being a proud grandmother: Jemma has a little boy called Gabriel. How rich life is.

. . . there are three things that last for ever: faith, hope and love; but the greatest of them all is love. *Corinthians, I*

Further Advice

I have mentioned throughout this book, *Love, Medicine and Miracles* by Dr Bernie S. Siegel (Arrow Books, 1989) as being very helpful. He has written two other books *Peace, Love and Healing* (Arrow Books, 1991) and *Living, Loving and Healing* (Aquarian Press, 1993). All worth buying.

Cancer Information at your Fingertips by Val Speechley and Maxine Rosenfield (Class Publishing, 1993) gives you clear, positive and practical information on cancer. It comes highly recommended by Roy Castle.

Gentle Giants by Penny Brohn, the co-founder of the Bristol Cancer Help Centre (Century Publishing Company, 1987), is a powerful story of one woman's unconventional struggle against breast cancer. A must for women who are interested, like Penny, in avoiding the conventional medical treatment offered, and in finding another path.

Bookshops are brimming over with helpful books on cancer, I recommend the ones mentioned above, but you will certainly be able to find the ones that suit you.

Finally, I would recommend a course of Aloe Vera juice and Aloe Vera tablets. The Aloe Vera plant is recognised as having health promoting qualities. Aloe Vera juice is widely used in hospitals in Russia as complementary to orthodox methods of treating cancer.

If you are interested, you can ask for a free information pack from: John Willcott, Osprey House, Haddenham Aerodrome, Haddenham, Buckinghamshire. Telephone: 01844 292 852.

Index